DIVYA SOOD

Find Someone to Love

ILOVEYOU

Find Someone to Love© 2019 by Divya Sood

For more information contact:
Riverdale Avenue Books/Magnus Imprint
5676 Riverdale Avenue
Riverdale, NY 10471
www.riverdaleavebooks.com

Design by www.formatting4U.com
Cover by Scott Carpenter
Digital ISBN: 9781626015029
Print ISBN: 9781626015036

First edition, May 2019

Dedication

For

My Baby who is a Rumi kind of girl

And for Mom, Dad, and Atul, always

DIVYA SOOD

Find Someone to Love

Between love and desire there is a place
I want to take you there
And place a finger upon your pink lips
And let you listen to my beating heart
That only knows your name
Between faith and belief there is a place
I want to take you there
And place my fingertips upon your eyelids
And let you listen to my voice
That speaks only your name
Between you and me there is a place
I want to take you there
And take my hands in yours
And stay there with you
With no distance between us
In an eternal embrace
I love you

Chapter One

It is one of those lazy days in July when even the air doesn't move. Dusk is sweeping into day and here I am, in a tiny studio bathroom in Queens, sitting on the edge of the bathtub, a half-smoked cigarette between the index and middle fingers of my left hand. The tip of the cigarette glows orange. Orange like the cloth of the priest that will pray for my cousin's soul before he hands a clay pot of ashes to my uncle so that he can set afloat the remains of his only son in the holy Ganges. Orange like the glow of the sun that will set on their day leading only to a night of "whys" and "hows" although the answers are not as mysterious as they hope.

I inhale from my cigarette and my mind tilts just a bit and a verse settles into my mind… "Tum rakshak kahoo ko darna?" It is from the 40 verses of the *Hanuman Chalisa*, this verse, and I can't shake it off for the life of me. She used to like his verse so much so that she took me to St. Mark's once, to a fading tattoo shop where she selected a bright orange ink to tattoo the verse onto her arm, an OM dangling from the last word. I would have chosen a fierce red with a black outline for something like that.

Red is my color, the color of the curves with which I have etched her name upon my wrist, a place where a

1

spray of perfume lands every morning, giving her name a fragrance. The fragrance of her memory sifts through days and nights to settle onto my soul and sometimes I want to talk to her, to say, "Let's try this again." But I cannot because she is not here and pursuing her at this point would be as futile as the tears I shed for a dead cousin while I sit on the rim of a bathtub, my cigarette now down to its last orange embers, my mind on fire with thoughts I haven't thought for years.

Years have gone by since I have seen him, since I have sat with him on a marble terrace, not talking, just taking in the wet monsoon air. We didn't need to speak, he and I because we had a connection that few could fathom, what with being born a day apart in the same hospital that sits near Bondel Road.

"What is his name, Prem?" I ask him without him ever telling me that there was a lover, that this lover had a name, and that this lover is now gone.

"Doesn't matter," he says, his eyes searching the horizon for comfort, the hazy green irises brightening with tears that I know he will never let fall.

I want to tell him that I have fantasies of my women too, to let him know this proclivity towards a common gender is not only his failing but mine too.

Upstairs, our parents share the common talk of marriage, of offers made and offers considered, wondering why he and I grudge the topic and keep silent when accosted with photos of prospects. I sometimes think his prospects would improve if he were to shift to New York instead of being confined to the city of Calcutta. If he could breathe, perhaps he could be. I imagine us during summer evenings, primed and dressed, ready for a night out at a sordid

2

club where the prospects are endless. But this, I know, is never to be. He is the only son and has been a good one, even running the failing coffee shop that is his father's misguided pride and joy.

Joy is a sensation I haven't felt for so long that when I try to remember the nuances of the word, it seems I have to navigate and negotiate so much memory that I lose myself. My last joy was a half-karat diamond on my ring finger, a thin gold band that she slipped past my knuckle as she knelt before me, sincere in her affection. Or so I thought. Who knows the workings of the chambers of the heart, how they endear a name at Christmas and forsake that same lover come Easter?

I could pretend I don't know why she left. Pretension is my forte. But my fort on this day is this small studio bathroom in Queens where I can stay secluded, ignore the fact that half a world away, three nights ago, a man hanged himself out of hopelessness. I can try to forget the fact that once a lover left me because my demons grew weary of my ineffectual attitude and started pawing at her and ultimately tried to destroy her instead. I can even try to rationalize how a woman I loved beyond reason never knew of my affection and all who followed, even those that gave me love, could never claim the beats of my heart as she had.

My memory is a sieve and all that has happened slips through to a floor of slippery consequences. But then the large recollections, the important dates and names and numbers, they get caught in the glistening mesh of this sieve and I remember. I remember the look her eyes held once on a cold winter's day at the end of January while she stood across from me, snowflakes catching in the curls of her hair, upon the

3

whims of her eyelashes. She had gone to England for the winter break. She had thought of me, she said, despite all that had happened, and had bought me a birthday gift that had remained in her maroon Jansport backpack through my birthday and long thereafter. But then somehow on this cold day in January, she had called, had said she needed to give me this present right away as if having it in her possession was burdening her, making the straps of the Jansport stretch and hurting her fragile back.

Back then, she had a boyfriend. He was a lanky 20 year-old who played basketball and failed calculus multiple times, a pseudo-poet who recited to her lines from Byron although I knew inside me that she was a Rumi kind of girl.

She held her hand out to me, a colorful cast of cartoons on the cover of the book she offered. I took it. Enid Blyton's *The Faraway Tree*.

"I searched for this, you know, through six shops and then some," she says in an English that is all her own, carried as was she in her mother's womb from Sri Lanka to Australia until finally, water broke, and she was born in the quaint city of Bahrain. The lilt of her words moves me, and I want her to speak more. I want her to talk to me even if to say that "he" is waiting for her, that she must depart, that she must leave me with my secret lust and boisterous denial of affection.

"Why did you get this for me?" I ask her although there is no answer she could ever offer that would be satisfactory leave "Because I love you" which is something I know she will never feel let alone say. It is I who love her, I who lie about it even to myself. We are young and just emerging. Although faint echoes of

4

Rumi whisper the refrain, "Lovers do not find each other somewhere /They are in each other all along." I wonder if I could ever enter her, not physically in that banal sort of way but through her eyes perhaps or through the lines of fate upon her palms, through her fingertips as they graze my hand, all in a trajectory that marks an ascent to her soul.

We have a habit of staring at each other and not speaking. It is just as quiet when we star gaze together not because we are star-crossed lovers but because we have both enrolled in Astronomy 101, her because she loves the stars, me because I have to fulfill a science requirement and biology intimidates me, the cutting of pig flesh and the pithing of frogs. Quietly, we stare at solemn skies, now and then jotting randomness on the college lined pages of our notebooks. These evenings I am smitten with her, pretend I don't see Orion's belt just so she can lean over me and point to the three stars that mark the hunter's waist. I inadvertently, or sometimes very knowingly, stretch my arms as she shows me Orion, my hand almost on her hips, almost grazing her skin where the rise of her shirt ends for she wears these shirts that leave her midriff bare, even in the winter, and it drives me crazy.

Those winter nights, our breath escaped us in puffs of smoke as we spoke of constellations and gaze at the heavens. I smoked sometimes and she never. And once when she saw me with a cigarette between my lips, she took it between her index finger and thumb and threw it to the ground.

"I care about you," she said, "don't ever do that again."

I would smoke a thousand cigarettes, I thought, if

5

the consequence of each was her face close to my own, the sound of her concern, her fingers close to my mouth. And then, after throwing the cigarette to the ground, her fingertips grazed my cheek, left impressions of affection somewhere upon my face, a friendly gesture that I wanted to mistake for something akin to love. Thereafter, I smoked more frequently, hoping to get caught. I became addicted instead, both to the cigarette dangling from my lips and to the woman dangling always in my periphery.

Peripheral vision is a fascinating concept, being aware of what is around as much as what is right in front of us. Around me, there were whispered words. Somehow it became important that I was president of Hindu Student Council, that I ran workshops on meditation. As if love for a woman was contentious to all that was Hindu, the pitting of affection against an entire religion.

She was my religion, the air I breathed, the ground beneath my feet, my hunger, my laughter, my goddess. I wondered then if my cousin's feet were cold as they were, most probably, jutting out from under a white sheet, small balls of white cotton stuffed into both his nostrils, prohibiting his soul from escaping from his nose for this was bad luck.

I envisioned the funeral which was occurring half a world away in a country half a day advanced. Time zones and a synchronicity and all of that nonsense. They had waited three days to cremate his body as they were waiting for relatives to arrive including me who made the excuse of work and stayed away not because I didn't care but because the idea of him without life was not acceptable to me.

As was I once upon a time when I first loved a Sri Lankan woman, to all those around me who saw as antonyms the words "Hindu" and "homosexual." They both began with a soft "h" and seemed innocent enough as words but then as realities rolled out into life, they did not seem to coexist. And if in a place as large and as extensive as Rutgers University those words were at odds, what if, what if by some random act of fate those word and notions were to enter the suspicion of those inside the realm of my household?

My dysfunctional household that consisted of a young aunt who was slightly retarded but not enough to solicit aid or sympathy; an old aunt that I was sure would never die and held notions such as that a woman should only eat after her husband has had a go at the plate, that the man should eat his fill, leave the bones of chicken and the fat of lamb for his wife's body to absorb; and then my parents who despised one another to the point of being madly in love because they could not tell the difference between love and hate, having been arranged to be married at 18 a piece, never having known affection or derision, nor acceptance or rejection. Two families entered an agreement and my parents were the pawns that moved across the chessboard of life except that they were given the rules to chess and expected to play backgammon.

It is a warm summer's evening when rain falls in slants outside the window of the dorm room and she and I are on the bed, sitting face-to-face, moving round discs around a backgammon board, talking of Bollywood and Hollywood and movies in between. She is wearing an orange tank top, a bright orange that could make my eyes smart if the room weren't so dull, so gray from the rain outside. She stretches out a hand to move a black disc and I discern her fragrance, a cheap scent called "Exclamation" that she probably purchased at a discount store somewhere and yet upon her skin the scent gains flavor and richness and desire.

I wonder what desires were within him when he died because he could not have died at 37 being desire-less and boring. Was there a lover for whom he spent his life? Or was there lack of a lover that led to his feeling suffocated before he suffocated himself, wrapped a rope around his larynx and swung back and forth in desperation?

He told me once of never wanting to be stuck in the life he lived. Perhaps he realized he couldn't escape any of it, the coffee shop, the talk of marriage, this finding and then releasing lovers at a stretch, not sure how to reconcile.

But then—then he reconciled or life was reconciled for him when his parents chose a bride, a sweet Bengali girl who committed to marriage and, in turn, abandoned her medical studies half way through.

We reconcile our backgammon pieces around the board, she watching the fate of white and black disks intently as I watch her, notice every angle of her layered hair, the flicker of her eyelashes.

"He wants to have sex," she says to me as if this revelation surprises me. As if this revelation does not tear me apart like a knife that separates two halves of a pomegranate, one half righteous and ripe and under-standing, the other naïve and jealous and wanting. I am both.

I pretend to concentrate on the black disk between my fingers although I can't count anymore, not even to add two plus two. But two plus two is always four and somehow this seems unfair all of a sudden. Just like it is unfair that he can hold her hand, kiss her skin where her forehead ends and her eyebrow curves into a solemn arch, just as he can easily say "I want sex" and I can't even imagine touching her hair, devoid of all nerves as it is.

"So, do it," I say as if to vindicate myself. I do not love her. I do not desire her. It is not I who can't make eye contact with myself in a mirror because her name lingers upon my lips long after I have no reason to utter the syllables that call her to me.

They used to utter it all under their breaths but now, now it is different. Now I have someone or the other come directly to me and ask, "Are you really in love with her?"

I shrug the question aside, say "no" very softly but emphatically. It is the same no my cousin uttered when his family sat him down, suggested he might be abnormal, offered drugs, treatment, electroshock therapy that cures men of the curse of loving other men.

He retreated brilliantly from their line of questioning, tore a page out of *Filmfare* featuring Dipika Padukone and professed his love to her, swore his love for all womankind.

It was only I that knew that torn from that same *Filmfare* was a poster of Ranvir Singh, hidden under a mattress, damp with desire.

Desire is a funny thing, catching in our throats when the only thing that should catch within us is duty and belonging. We are Indians, after all, not this race of "firungis" that our parents curse, this race that can't respect the elders and runs its own course amok. We are to bow to whims and acquiesce and then, suddenly, without our own knowledge, desire brims within us and changes the game, makes us utter dialogues such as "fuck the aunties" and nothing is the same ever again.

She changed me the minute I saw her standing at the student orientation desk, pushing her hair back with her right hand, writing the curves to her name with the left. A name that I would endear to me for years without realizing I was ever in love, professing a "friendship" until one day, sitting in a bathroom on the rim of a bathtub, I run out of cigarettes and ponder the death of a young 37 year-old man and think somehow of a monsoon-like summer when I was playing backgammon and finally, finally say out loud, "Shit, I was in love."

How could I ever expect anything to ever be the same again? The orange glow of the cigarette is long gone, and I inhale thinking I find in the stale bathroom air the scent of jasmine, the remnant of an incense stick glowing orange at the tip. Incense are lit in the evening time to pray, in the morning perhaps, definitely at prayers offered to the dead. And while I should concentrate on incense as they are probably being lit for the saving of his soul, I remember her hands clasping a brown stick to be lit, my hand cupping the tip and lighting it with a match, the semi-glow of her face in the orange flame.

"Jai Hanuman gyan gun sagar," she says with her eyes closed, "Jai kapish thehoo log ujagar." I listen to the couplets one by one until she finishes all 40 and starts softly singing an aarti, the sacred flame of a diya dancing on a plate she holds with both hands. And I slowly move to take the silver plate from her with the

10

diya resting on it but she doesn't hand it to me. She lets me place my hands over hers and we orchestrate clockwise circles of the plate together as she finishes the aarti and all that is within me is a fear I have never known until this verse from the *Chalisa* finds its way to me, "Tum rakshak kahoo ko darna?" I repeat the words and translate them to mean "If you are my protector, why should I be afraid?" And while I know I speak of Hanuman the magnificent, I can't help but want to whisper this one line of the 40 verses close to her ear so she can know that if she were to say, even softly, that this could be, that we could occur, then the fear within me would finally subside. Nothing of the sort happens. Her aarti ends, she holds the plate for me as I bless myself with the diya's sacred flame, and then she sets down the plate.

That night she will have sex with him and change our lives forever.

Chapter Two

The alarm sounded. I stretched back into my bed and closed my eyes as I transitioned my thoughts from her and him and to the day ahead. It was Tuesday which meant Sam would be coming by. I already heard him, his breathing heavy as he leaned forward over the makeshift profit and loss spreadsheet glowing on the computer.

"The business, " he would say, "the business needs more people to come in." He would say this as if "the business" were a living, breathing organism. Sometimes, I looked at him and wondered if he realized that this performance was stale, that I knew as well as he that all he was looking at was the positive cash flow that I created for him. But I humored him as I believed this to be the most important albeit hardest part of my job.

"Marketing," I would say.

"Ahhh… more money spent there, Priya. Give me solutions that don't eat up my money."

To this I would exhale slowly, audibly, pretending to think of alternatives.

He would spring forward and clasp his hands together before shouting "I got it!"

And then, then he would announce, "We'll run a promotion. That's it. People love a discount. Not even a discount, free stuff. People love free stuff."

His promotions were always a copy of one of the chain retail promotions. But he beamed as he announced them as if they were hatched in his mind were brilliant.

I had been working with Sam since the first day he took over the shady optical practice that used to be in place of the cozy optical we now have. The place used to be called O.M. Optical and was run by a young guy who made too much money and developed a cocaine addiction simply because he could afford it. He sold at a very fair price although Sam still insisted he could have gotten him to go lower.

When Sam took over the place, he changed the name to 20/20 Optical. He renovated the tacky orange and green theme to stark and clean white and black. When I met him for my interview, he was wearing a black Armani suit with a crisp pink shirt and tie. He struck me as someone who didn't just open a business but poured himself into it. He might not know it, but I rejected an offer at a major retail chain to work for him just because he spoke with such passion about what he was about to do.

It had been three years since that interview and now I was as devoted to 20/20 as Sam. Optical was a very interesting animal. If I were to assign a face to it, 20/20 would be a tiger cub. To look at it, the business seemed cute and playful. But to sell or go into the science of it, the potential was a roar, a fight, something vicious and yet beautiful and majestic.

I rose from my chair and showered, then changed into the black that Sam wants us all to wear to seem professional and yet somehow artistic. And then I left the apartment quietly, shutting the door behind me.

Chapter Three

My walk to work was my time, absorbed in music. My headphones let in no sound and while I was sometimes afraid that I would miss the screech of a horn and be dead, it was not enough of a fear for me to change my headphones or lower the volume. This morning though, I couldn't lose myself in lyrics. I kept thinking back to what I had been thinking, about the truth of it and about why it made my chest clench although so much time had passed. I didn't know what I wanted with the story, just that I wanted to write it, to share it, for anyone who would read it to know that once this woman existed.

I crossed the street when I reached the store and I let out a huge sigh. The gate was down. This meant that Ed hadn't arrived as he should have an hour before we opened to check and finalize jobs. This meant I would open in a rush and panic, reconcile the cash drawer, and begin checking jobs like a rabid dog hoping it wasn't busy until I finished. This was usual and customary but somehow it always managed to irk me.

What irked me more was that Sam never said a word to Ed. Never a reprimand, never a "be on time, buddy." Once I asked Sam why he let Ed slide as much as he did. Sam held up a pair of Kawasaki rimless frames with hi-index lenses in a minus six or six and a quarter, the lenses polished to a high sheen, the anti-reflection glinting green and maroon under the lights. It was beautiful, the edging, the drilling and the mounting.

"You see this?" Sam had said. "This is the work of a master. He's a master. He's the closest to the old-time guild opticians. His work is flawless. It's art. That's why, Priya. Is he late? Always late. Is he lazy? Like a sleeping dog. But does he do good work? The best. He's affordable. He does everything he has to. Maybe he only does it when he wants to. But he does it. And damn, what a job he does."

I couldn't argue with that. Sometimes, I was jealous of Ed. Not of his five o'clock shadow or his mumbling way of talking. Not of his ties that were always too short for his 6'1" frame nor of his too tight button downs that gapped to show a hairy belly and always managed to escape his pants no matter how many times he tucked them in. I was jealous of his knowledge, his skill. I sometimes wondered if I would ever know what he knew, be able to create what seemed like magic. Ed could take a plus four lens in poly, know to order it aspheric and cribbed, and edge it to a high polish knife-edge without a thought. I was lucky if I remembered half of all that. And I couldn't edge. Even with the press a button "it does it for you" machine, unless it was a straightforward prescription, I would manage to make it look ugly. The bevel would be in the wrong place. Or I would forget the polish. Ed never forgot the details.

What I envied Ed for most was his ability to make any prescription look beautiful. To make the seemingly ugly prescription transform into a work of art in his hands and through his work. I wished I could do that. And I knew I couldn't.

15

I turned the key and closed my eyes as I heard the sound of the shutter rise. I breathed deeply, ready for another day.

"Hey kiddo."

I opened my eyes and saw Ed, his transition lenses dark against the sun, his smile goofy and honest.

"Hey yourself. You're late."

"I know." He said. "I know."

I loved it that he never even tried to create an excuse.

Chapter Four

Sam was in a glum kind of mood when he entered the office. I was sitting at the desk, fidgeting with the nylon wire spool that we used for restrings. I had tried and failed for a half hour to restring a rectangular minus eight lens into a thin gold semi-rimless until finally Ed had gently taken it from my hand and restrung it in less than five minutes, softly lecturing me the entire time in his soft voice that was both encouraging yet tinged with disappointment.

"Measure once, cut twice." He said. "You cut the wire too small. That's why it won't go in. Always measure a thousand times before you cut."

He pried the wire free of the metal and inserted new nylon into the small holes, weaving as if he had done this a million times which I was sure he had in the 30 years he had surrounded himself with eyeglasses.

"And you always want to go from temple to nasal when you slide the ribbon under," he said.

"Yes, I know but it wouldn't fit."

"The wire was too short, kiddo. As you do this more, you'll judge better."

"Who wears a semi-rimless in a minus eight anyway?" I countered. I wore a slight pout of embarrassment.

"People want what they want. Can't help that."

I took the spool of nylon in my hand and wound and unwound the end.

"Sam's coming." I said. "I'm going to the office."

So that's how I was in the office playing with nylon wire, wondering if I would ever be able to work with the ease and facility that Ed did.

"How's the book looking?" Sam asked.

"We have a few appointments," I said.

"What's a few? Three? Six?"

"Five. But we could have walk-ins. And the doctor is leaving early so I can't book the evening."

Sam sighed.

"Why is she leaving early today?"

"I don't know. She just said no appointments after four."

He placed his hands behind his neck and laced his fingers.

"I am thinking of a new doctor," he said.

"What do you mean? Get rid of her?"

He unlaced his fingers, placed his hands on the desk across from me, and then intertwined them again, his left thumb resting on top.

"Priya, she leaves early more than I do. She has no regard for the business."

He opened his hands and lowered his head so his eyes rest on his palms.

"And she wants a raise."

I laughed. I didn't mean to laugh but it really was ludicrous. He was right about the doctor wanting to leave early on any given day for no known reason. He was also right that she wasn't concerned about the business. But a raise? I didn't blame his agitation or his despair.

"We'll find someone," I said.

"Who? I mean I want to tell her to just go. But I can't leave the business dark. I need a doctor for this place. So, either I come up with a raise or risk not having a doctor at all."

"Go to SUNY." I said. "Tons of fresh grads who'll die for a place like yours."

He looked up and smiled.

"You think they'd DIE for a place like ours?"

The fact that he said "ours" made me smile back at him.

"Sam, you have a great place. Just go out there and find someone to love it."

He sat back and exhaled loudly.

"I have a friend who is a professor over at SUNY. I think I'll call him for leads. I don't want a newbie either, Priya. I want someone who has done this. Someone who has passion. Someone who is… hungry."

"No one is as hungry as you, Sam. But if that's what you want, I'm sure it'll work out."

"You always make me feel better."

"That's why I'm here."

I didn't really know why I was there or how I had become such an integral part of the place. I graduated with a Master of Arts in English. English. And somehow, along the way, between undergraduate and graduate schools, I'd gotten mesmerized by the world of optics and had spent two years soul searching while earning a degree in Ophthalmic Dispensing. I took the state exam on a whim and there I was, a bona-fide licensed optician in the state of New York.

I never intended to use my license. I pursued English in graduate school dreaming of glamorous jobs in advertising or magazine editing. But then upon graduating and working at a start-up medical magazine, I realized it was too much work for too little pay. And when the magazine failed, I slipped easily into optical where with the skills I had, there was money to be made.

More than money, I enjoyed the entertainment of it. I enjoyed the stories of the people I worked with and the people I serviced. I enjoyed seeing new faces every day, the excitement of a sale, the look of awe when a pair of glasses was close to God-like perfection. Somehow, I enjoyed it more than I thought I would.

But beyond the optical haven that we had created and adored, I still wanted to write a story. The story. Her story. And mine. Except every time I tried, it ended with a blank page and the cursor line blinking at me. Somehow, our story felt incomplete. And there seemed no point in chasing ghosts from the past.

"I'm going to give her another two weeks to see how she does," Sam said, interrupting my thoughts.

"What do you think is going to change?"

He shrugged and leaned back in his chair.

"I like giving a fair shake."

"So, are you going to talk to her and tell her she has to change the way she is?"

"Call her in here."

I pressed the phone intercom button to the front.

"Yeah?" Ed said as if he were being disturbed.

"Is the doctor with a patient?"

"No."

"Can you send her in here please?"

"I would," Ed answered, "but she just stepped out for a minute."

"To where?"

"She had to exchange a shirt or skirt or something.

20

Wait, she's coming towards the door now. I'll send her in."

I released the intercom and stared at Sam who was shaking his head.

"Exchange a shirt or skirt or something? Now? See, that's what I'm talking about."

"I know."

There was a slight knock on the door. Sam cleared his throat and bellowed, "Come in."

Dr. Bello walked in with the grace and power that she kept for occasions such as these. She was the only person in the office who was exempt from the "wear all black" rule. Sam said it was because she wore a doctor's coat anyway. I believed it was because he liked the way she looked in color and that he was too scared to impose his dress code on her.

Beneath her pressed white coat, Dr. Bello had on a lilac skirt with a slight shimmer. Her blouse had swirls of dark purple and white and dipped generously at her cleavage. Her stockings were net and her heels must have been six-inch pencil heels in a patent leather white. When she smiled at Sam, I knew the conversation was not going to have any result. The thing was, Sam could talk a good game to me but as soon as she charmed him with her smile consciously and with the lilt of her perfume unconsciously, Sam was no longer strong. It wasn't that he melted (that's so cliché anyway) but he softened.

"Dr. Bello." He said.

"Yes, Sam?"

"Dr. Bello, why are we leaving early today?"

She slowly placed her left hand in her hair and massaged her scalp.

"I have a date."

"And abandoning your practice for a date seems fair to you?"

I looked at Sam in shock. He wasn't softening. He wasn't losing ground. I realized he was done with her antics. It excited me. It also scared me as I knew that he was taking a gamble.

"Sam, I have a personal life. And this is not my practice. It's yours. I work here to make you lots of money."

"You also make lots of money, Dr. Bello."

"Not enough. Which is something I wanted to talk to you about."

She looked at me and smiled slightly. She nodded in acknowledgement that I was there. I think she saw me as somewhat of a nuisance most of the time.

"Dr. Bello, we have spoken about this. You make one and a half times what the average OD makes in a practice of this size."

"And I am twice as good."

"When you are here. When you aren't frolicking around returning skirts."

She moved a step back.

"Well, Sam, if you're not happy with the way I work, I can go elsewhere. Start tomorrow. Anyone will be happy to have me. You can kiss all my credentialing goodbye and find a new OD who will take months to be credentialed by all these insurance companies. In the meantime, you can lose more money than if you just paid me what I wanted and respected me."

"I respect you! It is you who don't respect me. Or this practice."

Dr. Bello swallowed and then formed her lips into a thin line as if offering sympathy.

"I'm so sorry you feel that way, Sam."

Sam was breathing audibly and faster. I had never seen him so determined or so frustrated.

"Should I start looking?" she asked.

Sam locked eyes with her and she didn't flinch. Eventually, she slowly lowered her lids to blink, her mascara perfect and her eye shadow blended slightly at the corners of her smoky eyes. It was a deliberate, sultry blink. She knew. But she didn't know that I knew it.

"Dr. Bello, there are two and a half weeks left of this month. Let us see what the numbers say. How many appointments there are. How the business does. At that time, we can have a further discussion."

"As you wish, Sam. I am leaving at four today. No appointments after 3:15."

With that she turned and turned the knob. She shut the door behind her.

"What was that?" I asked.

"Yeah, she's got this attitude that she's God's gift to optometry—"

"No, Sam, you. What's gotten into you? I've never seen you that upset with her."

Sam looked around the room. There were papers strewn on the filing cabinet, coffee cup rings on the desk which was bare except for a blotter.

"I want the business to grow." he said. "I can't anymore. At first, I believed her hype about being better than the best. But I don't see it anymore, Priya. And then the raise. Do you know how much she would be making? Even with a new doctor and credentialing, it beats… it beats this."

I cracked my knuckles and looked at my dry hands.

I looked up and followed Sam's gaze to the corner of the room. There stood a small statue of Hanuman that I had presented him with when the store opened.

"What does your monkey God say to all this?" he asked.

I laughed, relieved that the tension was dissipated.

"He says be strong. He will see you through."

"Then Priya, let's start OD hunting."

He hit the table with his fist for emphasis.

"I'm going to contact my friend at SUNY. We can do this."

"Yes we can, Sam. And we will."

Sam and I went for lunch at the corner Thai restaurant. After that he left and I went back to a day with Ed and the doctor and patients until she left exactly at 3:59 p.m. I knew this because I checked my phone as her heels clattered on the hardwood and the bells on the door jingled in a ruckus when she pushed too hard. Ed looked at me and smirked.

"Wish I had a job like that," he said.

"So do I." I said. "So do I."

Chapter Five

I slowly sip some green tea and think back to the day. I remind myself that I have to change the frame on order 1451 because Mr. Goddard called at 7:05 to tell me that he wanted the black frame, not the brown because his wife ultimately decided it accented his blue eyes better. I thought back to his bushy gray eyebrows and the jutting bone of his forehead, his ample nose, and wondered if anyone ever noticed his eyes anyway. But I acquiesced and graciously agreed to switch the frame which I had not done because I was on my way out, Ed breathing sharply beside me, his finger raised to detonate the alarm system with a code he usually forgot twice or thrice before he set the alarm.

I wondered who would replace Dr. Bello, if anyone. Sam had run-ins with her constantly, but she was still there, three years strong. But now, it seemed he had hardened his resolve. I wondered if every person, every idea, every living and non-living thing had a breaking point. My cousin did although I would never know what that was. And she, Leyla, she did. Although I wish she hadn't, because I so loved her, I never wanted any piece of her or her life to break. But it did. At least once. Of that I am sure.

I placed my empty cup in the sink, sank into my makeshift writing chair, and started to type.

It was a deceptively blazing day in March. The sun had not shone all morning and the sky was a gloomy gray, but the morning was scorching. I was lying in my sheets trying to find the coolness of the bed which was hot and weighted with sleep. The air conditioner was on but not high enough and I debated turning it higher but never did because rising out of bed might mean rising for the day and I didn't want that just yet.

I was lucky enough to have an apartment adjacent to campus because my parents believed it would lead to better concentration and study than sharing a space with strangers. I in turn decided during the second semester of my freshman year that I wouldn't study biology and calculus, that I would shun the pre-med and embrace liberal arts. I became, to the shame and disappointment of my parents, an English major. Such an unfortunate turn of events, really. I turned and lay still with my eyes open, held my breath to see how long I could sustain an inward intake of air.

The buzzer sounded harshly, and I exhaled all too much and loudly. I looked at my phone and it was half past seven. On a Sunday.

When I opened the door, she was there. Her royal blue tank and white shorts gave her a playful look. Her hair was swept into a loose ponytail. Beads of sweat made her forehead and shoulders shimmer. I looked down at first, embarrassed at my pale paisley boxers and oversized plain red T-shirt. She should have called to say she was coming. Or arranged a time better than half-past seven on a Sunday when I was too casual and half asleep.

"It's so hot!" She said as she brushed past me and into the apartment.

She turned on the faucet, swiveling the handle to the hot side of the water and started soaping a sponge to wash the few dishes in the sink. I would have stopped her, but I was anticipating her words. Why was she at my apartment? What was she about to spill into my life and heart that would make everything somersault as it so often did when she released parts of herself into my sphere?

"What's going on?" I asked as nonchalantly as possible.

"Nothing. I just thought I'd stop by. See if you wanted breakfast. I slept with him."

Breakfast. I tried to think and keep my mind at bagels or eggs or cereal as mundane as that was. My mind did not stop there. *I slept with him.* What did that mean really? I tried not to think. I tried not to feel. She had a strand of hair on her cheek and she must have felt the tickle. She tried to move with it her forearm, her hands soapy and glistening with water. I used the index finger and thumb of my left hand to move the hair away, careful not to touch her cheek, knowing the whole while that if I did, my hand might open and my palm would want to rest there, to feel the brownness of her skin under my paler skin, to absorb her soul in a touch.

"How was it?" I asked.

She did not look at me. She looked instead at the sponge as if it would metamorphose in her hand into something different.

"I bled," she said.

I didn't want to know. Me, who had never been that close to another, man or woman, I didn't want to know. I didn't want to think of her with him. With anyone. Not even me. She was someone to be worshipped, someone to be kept in a distant altar. Perhaps I would touch her feet with my right hand and bring my hand to my forehead, slowly to my heart. Perhaps I would use both hands to touch the ground in front of her feet and bring my fingertips to my closed eyes. These were the forms of worship that I knew and adored, the rituals that were deserving of the gods. Deserving of her. Since when do we fuck our deities?

It was a powerful word, fuck. It held in its forearms my anger, my jealousy, my rage. But it was not just the act of. It was that she was still vibrating with thoughts of the act. She was talking about it, engulfed in moments I could not know, in moments I did not and could not ever share.

How can we ever share the intimacies of another's intimacies, the most guarded and sacred and secret places being the mind and heart? I thought back to my cousin and wished for the seconds that it took me to conjure the thought that I knew what made him decide to mark the end of a life. His life stained with the faith and love of those who knew him and the admiration and infatuation of those who didn't. It wasn't reversible, suicide. Did he know that? Was he aware? Or was he so caught up in the moment, the measurement of the rope, the calculation of the distance between the chair and the fan that he didn't stop to think once about consequence.

Everything had a consequence. My decision to forsake medical school had a consequence I did not foresee. While I enrolled in classes for Shakespeare and Milton, she was there, enrolling in biochemistry and physics. I would have known her sooner had I also pursued science. But when we meet and how we meet is a science dictated by fate and happenstance. And of course, consequence.

When I met her, it was towards the beginning of my junior year and I had more than half my liberal arts credits tucked away. She was well on her way to graduation as well although she was a year younger than me. But she was years smarter. When it came to memorization and formulas, her mind was nimble and adept and maneuvered deftly. My mind lingered, analyzed, traveled through tunnels of conflict and questioning. We were both best suited for what we chose to pursue in life. Although if I had stayed course true to my parents' yearnings, I would have met her sooner. We would have had different conversations, more of them. Or perhaps the consequence would have been that we would have met and nodded, smiled across classrooms and lecture halls but never become what we finally became: friends.

I met her at the student center one afternoon as I was shooting pool to ready myself for a midterm exam. I always shot pool before an exam as the concentration of it allowed what I had read and studied to ferment and to seep into me. At least that is what I believed and being that I was more than halfway through college with a perfect grade point average, I believed there must have been some truth or validity to my method. I shot the eight ball into the corner pocket, my method of always standing slightly off to the right seeming to work quite well. The ball rotated in the mouth the pocket few times with some velocity and then I heard it traveling through the tunnel of the table.

When I straightened, she was standing there, just beyond where the eight ball had sunk. She was smiling, admiring my lucky shot, believing me to be more talented at pool and at life than I ever was or would be.

"Can I watch you?" she asked.

"You can play with me," I responded.

This exchange would be the foreshadowing of our acquaintance and of our friendship.

I didn't even ask her name as I took the balls, two at a time and racked them within the triangle.

"I'm Leyla," she offered.

"I'm Priya," I accepted.

We played silently, and she was no good. I wasn't good either but that afternoon, I was lucky and so it made me look as if I were good at the game.

The silence in which we played seemed like a game to me, yet I know now and I knew even then I think that it was not for her. She was merely being Leyla, offering her name and her time to someone she didn't know. It was this quality about her that drew me to her, kept me drawn to her, and then angered me about her. How quickly she endeared herself to strangers only to leave them wanting more than she would ever proffer. How quickly she endeared herself to me.

"I can never make this shot," she finally said.

"That's because you're left-handed. I'm right-handed so I can make it."

She looked at me over the length of the pool stick. I walked over to her side of the table.

"Let me show you."

I placed a hand over hers and arched over her to find her other hand on the end of the pool stick.

There was a current that surged through me as I touched the tops of her hands. I let go in fear of being consumed by it, burned to nothing more than ash. She stood and looked at me.

"Why did you let go?" she asked.

"Just giving you some space."

I walked quickly over to the other side of the table and remained there waiting for her to shoot and miss. She shot, and the ball slowly rolled and rolled and stopped short of the pocket.

"If you had kept holding, I would have made the shot," she said.

"Sorry?"

"Why did you let me go?"

It seemed a dialogue fit for friends. For lovers. Not necessarily for two random students who happened to share a game of pool.

"Told you. Just giving you some space."

I started to chalk the stick and looked hard at the blue chalk. I felt my face was hot. I knew my face was reddening. I hoped she didn't notice.

"Are you angry?" she asked.

I looked up from the chalk to meet her gaze. She had drawn her eyeliner to extend beyond the corners of her eyes. Her eyes were a light hazel, much lighter than mine.

"No, I'm not angry. Why?"

"You're turning red."

Chapter Six

"There are many different types of anti-reflection," I said to the woman across from me. She was new to the area and had found us unexpectedly while walking her black poodle who now sat at her feet, his tongue hanging out as he breathed rather loudly. She herself was dainty and looked as if she belonged on the Upper East side of Manhattan, not at a corner optical in Jackson Heights. But she had moved here she said because Manhattan was too overrated. I didn't quite know what that meant but I knew she was not going to make a purchase before having a detailed conversation all the while being as supercilious as she could be.

"What are the differences?" she asked.

She enunciated each syllable of her speech.

"Well, for example, there is anti-glare to block blue light. It blocks glare, of course. But it's also a therapeutic lens. It slows the progression of cataracts and macular degeneration."

"Cataracts? How old do you think I am, dear?"

"Cataracts develop over time, Ms. Hoffman. It has nothing to do with being old."

I could see this sale would take some time and my only hope was to stay my course, to keep maintaining eye contact and to not look away or flinch. If I looked away or if I didn't have a comeback to her remarks, I would lose her. I knew that.

Ed stood at the counter behind me. I could not see him, but I knew he was leaning there, smiling.

"And light isn't blue, you know," she said. "Neither is the sky."

"No, light is not blue, it is a spectrum," I countered. "But there is a wavelength of blue and that causes damage. But if you prefer not to have a blue light blocking non-glare, we can look at other types."

"So, you don't want me to have the best?" she queried.

Here I paused, reassessing my strategy. My eyes stayed locked with hers. Her eyes were a pale blue and had a sharpness to them. Her skin was taut and although she wasn't old as she had said, I knew she was over 60 because I had read her check-in paperwork.

"I want you to have the best," I finally said.

"So then tell me, what is the best?"

"What activities do you enjoy, Ms. Hoffman? The best is what makes you comfortable and suits your lifestyle needs."

Lifestyle needs. That seemed fair.

"I jog. But I do not jog with glasses. I paint. Acrylic. For that I wear them. I read the paper. *The New York Times*. Oh, their print is so small. It's infuriating. For that I wear my glasses. I do not watch commercial television, but I do watch documentaries at times. For that I wear them. And I read books. I wear them all the time actually. Except when I jog."

"What's the lighting like where you paint?"

"Oh, you know, it gets to me sometimes, the brightness of my studio."

"Based on what you are telling me, you should definitely have anti-reflection. Let's discuss options."

The anti-reflection dilemma lasted over half an hour until she finally did select the blue light blocking treatment that I had initially suggested. Then we moved onto a discussion about progressive options which lasted well over 45 minutes. Usually, I would have completed three sales in this time. But she was meticulous, the store was empty, and I knew she would be buying at least two pairs and it was worth my investment of time. I also knew that if she liked me and my service, she would return whenever it was her whim to buy. She told me at one point that she bought glasses frequently depending on her mood. I wanted her mood to direct her back to our store as often as she wanted a new pair of glasses.

I took the first pair she had selected, a stylish black and gold Dior.

"Put these on for me please," I said.

She put them on with her fingertips.

"Now are they comfortable where they are?"

"Well, give me a moment. I just put them on."

I waited as she fiddled with the frame on her fine bridge. She looked in the oval mirror beside her. Fiddled some more.

"How do they look?" she asked.

"Perfect."

"Well carry on then."

I used a black marking pen to dot the lenses where her pupils were.

"There we go. You can take them off now."

"That's it?"

"Yes, Ms. Hoffman."

"Well that's not very scientific now, is it?"

"It's most accurate," I said.

We repeated the process with her second pair, a tortoise Fendi.

After I wrote all her measurements on the invoices, it came time for the payment. Although most times I dreaded announcing the total, with her, I was unafraid. I knew my work was done and if I had gotten this far, she would offer me a credit card and pay in full with no argument or feigned shock.

I was right. When I announced her four-digit total, she simply reached into her Gucci clutch and handed me a card. I took her card slowly and almost unenthusiastically as if payment was the last thing on my mind. I rose and went to the credit card terminal and swiped. Approved. Of course, it would be. I took her receipts back to her and she signed as if she were graciously giving me an autograph.

"Thank you, Ms. Hoffman. They should be ready in seven to 10 business days if not sooner. We will call you."

"And what was your name again?"

"Priya."

"Is that Indian?"

"Yes, it is."

"Ah, beautiful country India. I went once you know. Beautiful people. Just a shame about the poverty."

I nodded.

"Well, it was a pleasure."

She rose from her seat."

"Come now, Compton," she said to the poodle.

Compton readily followed her out, his tongue still hanging, his breathing still loud. She opened the door softly and the bells were almost still as the door shut with only a slight jingle.

"That was impressive, kiddo," Ed said as he walked over to my seat. "You could sell ice to a polar bear."

"It wasn't too bad."

"I can never sell like that. Don't have the patience for it."

"But you can spend an hour assembling a drill mount. See I don't have the patience for that."

"That's why we're a team, kiddo. We work well together."

We did work well together. Our days were usually silent save a conversation about glasses or the business as Ed was not a talker. I wondered if it was because he was lost in thought most of the time or because he really had nothing to talk about. But I was sure he had a story or two. All I knew was that he had enlisted in the army at 26 and stayed for 10 years. I wondered sometimes though about his heart. About his having loved or been loved. But Ed was like a father to me and it was awkward asking those questions. So, I never asked. And he never mentioned.

I sometimes wanted to tell him how grateful I was for him despite his being late and lazy most of the time. I didn't even mind having to direct him or tell him what to do because his eyes usually looked lost and he acted as if he truly didn't know what to do next even if there were jobs piled for final inspection or to be ordered. I actually enjoyed guiding him through his day. It made me feel useful. And he always seemed grateful with a lopsided grin and a "Thanks, kiddo" ready to spill from him.

"You want lunch?" Ed asked. "My treat."

"Why?"

"Just because."

There it was, the signature Ed, the lopsided grin and a brightness in his eyes as if he were going to do something mischievous.

"Sure. What would you like?"

"No, no, no. It's my treat. Anything you want."

"Chicken biryani?"

I chose biryani because in Jackson Heights, you couldn't go wrong with Indian food. But I also chose it because although it was just a meal for me, chicken biryani, it was Ed's favorite dish in the entire world.

"If that's what you want."

He gently touched my head as he headed out to get the food.

I wanted to hear his stories. I thought to ask him when he returned. Not about his entire life, just about the time before the army. What had he done? How had he lived?

Ed came in with a harsh jangle of bells. He always flung the door wide open when he entered. He set the food down on the reception counter.

"No one's coming in on doctor's lunch," he said. "We can eat out here."

If Sam were there, he would have balked at us eating on the floor. But he wasn't. And I wasn't about to argue because I was really hungry.

We ate behind the front desk, quietly. The doctor was in her office and I would have offered her some food, but she had the door closed which meant she was not to be disturbed. She did this often and I often wondered what she did in the dark room all by herself. Of course, I never asked, and she never told us.

Ed had a hearty appetite and he knew it so he had gotten two plates of chicken biryani for us although usually, one plate would have easily fed two people. I watched him eat from the tin foil container without pause. I thought it time to ask what I believed was quite a harmless question.

"Ed?"

He nodded with his mouth full.

"What did you do before this?"

He looked at me quizzically. He swallowed then took a sip of water from a bottle.

"I told you, I was in the army."

"But before that?" I asked. "You joined the army at 26. What did you do before that?"

He set down the bottle and his head bent just a bit. When he looked up, he looked directly into my eyes. His stare was distant.

"I was married," he said. "I was working on Wall Street."

"Married? What was she like? Where did she go?"

"She was perfect. She was five years older than me. When I was 25, she died. I spent a year in a dark apartment drinking. And then I enlisted."

I was at a loss. I wanted to hear stories, not five sentences about how his life had completely changed from hope to despair. I didn't know what to say to him.

"Kiddo?"

"Yeah?"

"Let's just eat the biryani."

And we ate in silence.

Chapter Seven

Sam kicked in the door at about half past five, the bells crashing together as he did. His hands were full with his laptop and vanilla colored file folders threatening to spill papers everywhere. In his mouth, he held tightly to a piece of paper that flapped as he entered. I was with a patient when he came in and my eyes looked up to meet his. He nodded at me and the paper moved up and down. Instead of retreating to his office, he set down his files and laptop on an empty desk and took the paper out of his mouth. He stood there, and I knew he was listening to me. He did that often. I guessed he should just to make sure I was doing everything I could to perform to his standards. Sam had exceptionally high standards when it came to sales. That's a lot of the reason I respected him. He loved the money and he was greedy, but he was ethical, and I felt he really wanted to provide the best.

"So, I only want what my insurance covers," the man was saying.

"Yes, Mr. Gomez—"

"Call me Rocco."

"Yes, Rocco, but you see your prescription is a minus ten in one eye, a minus eight in the other."

"I don't understand a word of what you just said, Piya."

"Priya. It's Priya."

"Whatever, listen, I don't want to pay a penny, not one penny" he said as he threw the frame he had chosen across the desk. "I pay enough for this insurance and I'm not paying a thing. And you're talking nonsense that I don't understand."

"I apologize." I said. "So, let me explain it better, Rocco."

"Okay… "

"You wear contacts. I get that. You haven't bought glasses since high school. I get that. What I'm saying is, you can't see. Your prescription, what you need to see, will be so thick in what the insurance covers that you'll hate it. It'll be thick. Very thick. Reflections everywhere. I just want what's best for you. All I'm asking you to do is pay a slight, a very slight copayment for a thinner lens. And anti-glare. That's all."

Rocco shifted in his chair. He cleared his throat. I knew I at least had him thinking. I hoped he would understand or else he would return, hate the glasses, and accuse me of not telling him how horrendous the glasses would be.

"Slight copayment?"

"Yes." I said.

"And they'll look better than if I just take the crap the insurance gives me?"

"Much better. I mean they can't be paper thin because you do have a high prescription. But if you don't, they'll be really, really awful."

He sighed. He stared at the frames as if they would respond or make a decision for him. He picked them up and bent the temples back and forth. Then he threw the frames towards me onto the table.

"Okay. Okay, just do whatever you have to. My meter's about to expire."

I quickly wrote the frame details, the lens details, jotted his pupillary distance, and took the cash from him.

"Thank you, Rocco. I'll call you personally when these are ready."

"You got my money," he said as he stood and zipped his Ralph Lauren windbreaker. He had an awful smile. It was predatory, like the wolf in Red Riding Hood.

"You're investing in a great pair of glasses," I said.

"Yeah, yeah. I know what these things cost you guys. You're milking it."

With that comment, Rocco turned, brushed past Sam, and left.

"Good job, Piya," Sam said as he smiled and clapped a few slow claps.

"Shut up, Sam."

"You got my money," he imitated. "You got my money."

"Sam, how the hell can I sell the guy plastic lenses? Is he for real?"

"That's why you are the professional in this equation. Where's Ed?"

"He went to get a snack."

"How much can that guy eat? Does he have a tapeworm?"

"Come on, Sam. He's a big guy."

Sam squared his shoulders and stood taller.

"Well when he returns, kindly join me in the office. I have something to share with you."

41

I realized I had hurt his pride with the "big guy" comment. Sam was very sensitive about his slight belly and stocky frame. He stood at a clean 5'7" and yet swore he was 5'9" but seemed shorter because he was a bit pudgy. He also swore to get to the gym and back to his college body yet in three years, all that accomplished was him paying exorbitant gym fees to a place he had only entered for orientation.

"You look nice today," I said.

Sam grunted as he picked up his laptop and papers.

"Nice try," he retorted as he shuffled to his office.

When Ed came back, he held a cup overflowing with vanilla frozen yogurt, strawberries, and chocolate syrup.

"Eating healthy," he said as he used the little red plastic spoon to push a heap of yogurt into his mouth. A bit of the syrup dripped onto his white shirt.

"Oh fuck," he said as he used his finger to smear the syrup thereby making the stain larger instead of cleaning it off.

"I have to go talk to Sam," I said.

"Sam's here? Did he ask where I was?"

"Yes and yes. But when I told him you went for a snack, he totally understood."

Why Ed acted as if Sam would ever say anything about his whereabouts was beyond me. But he was always a bit paranoid that Sam would reprimand him. I watched him set down his yogurt and fidget with the stain on his shirt. I wondered about his dead wife and his life before the army, before the world of optical bliss.

"I'm going to the back," I said.

He nodded, too preoccupied with his shirt to say anything.

I knocked on Sam's door. He didn't open the door. I heard him talking. Usually, he kept his door flung wide open, even when he was on the phone. I wondered what was different now.

"Sam?"

"On the phone," he replied.

He wasn't going to let me know about this one. It was very unlike him. Sam trusted me with every detail of his life from how much he owed a vendor to a woman he met at a bar and spent the night with. There were no secrets in his world and I was dying of curiosity about who he was talking to. Just as I raised my hand to knock again, he opened the door.

"Priya! Come in."

He shut the door behind us.

"What's going on?" I asked.

"Priya, Priya, Priya. I have just made one of the most sound business decisions of my life."

"As in?"

"As in I hired a new doctor."

I stared at his face. He wasn't joking.

"What do you mean?"

"I'm telling Dr. Bello that she has two weeks. And then we start a new chapter here at 20/20."

"Who? How?"

Sam reclined back in his chair and laced his fingers behind his head. His green eyes swam in joy and he seemed, for once, relaxed.

"My friend at SUNY. He had someone. I talked to her. I met him and her for lunch the other day. Beautiful woman. And reasonable. Very reasonable.

Yes, we'll have to suck it up until she's credentialed with all the insurances. But I think it'll be worth it."

"Wow, Sam. You did it."

"I did indeed. Priya, nothing but smooth sailing from here on out."

I smiled and Sam winked at me. He was wearing a pale olive shirt and it made his eyes seem brighter. Or maybe his eyes were brighter because there was something about him that was different when he spoke of the change. I hoped the new doctor would put his mind at ease and that she would be everything he hoped.

"Well, Sam, I'm happy for you."

"For us," he said. "For us.

Chapter Eight

Monsoon rain left me ambivalent. There were times I loved the fury of the clouds and the insistence of the rain as it swelled and swallowed Calcutta whole. And yet there were times I wished it would stop and not show off all its majesty. That summer, the rains were unstoppable. It was the last summer I would see him alive or otherwise but I did not know that at the time. It was a particularly dark monsoon afternoon when we sat just inside the verandah, despite admonishment that the glass of the door might shatter and hurt us. But nothing was hurting us and we were brave. In the background, Sting was singing of jealous winds. He loved Sting. And Springsteen. He swore he was meant to be a blue-eyed blonde somewhere in America and not a brown-eyed boy in Calcutta. But there he was with me, ankles crossed, knees bent to his chest, sitting on the floor and rocking slightly, his arms encircling his shins. He smiled. That is what I remember now. The peace and piece of a smile that was perhaps not contentment.

"Do you think I could ever go to America?" he asked earnestly, eagerly.

"Why not?"

He looked at the floor, a stray cockroach scuttling

about until it disappeared through a crevice to the verandah.

"Are there cockroaches in America then?"

"Yes," I said.

"But still, I want to go there. To be free."

What he wanted to be free of I wasn't sure. Perhaps the dismal coffee shop he was forced to run despite his triumph in engineering. But he had not finished the program because he was, if not wanted, then desperately needed to heed the duties of a family that was falling into slight despair.

"What do you want in life?"

He stared concertedly through the glass, the rain making the sight outside blurry, the darkness not warranting a clear view.

"I want to be happy." He finally said. "But I don't know what that feels like. And I don't know if I would know it if I ever found it."

I wondered what he had found close to death. I wondered if it was the breaking and cracking of despair or an elation that he would no longer be where he wished not to be. These were questions I knew would never be answered and so they lingered and gnawed me much like a dull pain that you get used to although you wish it were not there.

She lingered outside his dormitory building and wondered if she should ring the bell to alert him of her presence. This is before he liked her, before the relationship and the sex and the ensuing madness that engulfed our lives like flames of ice.

"What is the big deal?" I asked.

She looked at me in such a way as to say she herself didn't know. It was a blank look I thought yet if I were honest, it was a look that spoke of the fact that all that preoccupied her thoughts and her heart was the notion of seeing him. I didn't want to face that honesty because it stirred my own heart and I needed not to be stirred.

"Don't leave," she said.

"I'm not leaving but standing here just dawdling makes no sense either."

"I want to see him but what will I say? I can't tell him I want to see him."

I lit a cigarette with the hopes of having it extinguished by her fingers. Nothing of the sort happened. I inhaled and exhaled slowly as she stared at the black buzzer button as if it would react.

"Just ring the damn bell," I said.

My agitation caused her to jump.

"You can go if you want to," she countered, not with aggression, but in defeat.

I looked towards the sky, swirls of gray marking imminent rain. Not a monsoon for sure but an annoying mist of moisture that would be cold and uncomfortable.

"I won't," I said. "I won't just leave you."

I threw the butt to the ground and stepped on it, disappointed that I had finished, and she had not even noticed.

"Why don't you ring the bell and tell him you came to borrow something? Then start talking to him about random things."

She pondered this tactic. Then her lips parted in a smile just as the rain started a slow descent from the sky.

"Brilliant," she said when it really wasn't brilliant.

With a step, she came close and put her arms around my shoulders in a slight hug. I inhaled and the intonation of her perfume was caught within me. My arms stayed at my sides because I think I knew that if I were to hold her, my fingers would travel the length of her hair only to stop at the slenderness of her neck. I could not risk such outlandish and dangerous actions.

When she stepped back, I finally released my breath without realizing that I had been holding it within my chest for all the while that she held me.

As the rain silently reached us, she pressed the buzzer. I looked away as if hers was an intimate gesture. In the distance, past the haze of rain, I saw a slight rainbow, not a work of nature but a slight small flag with a wooden stick held by someone who was obtaining signatures on a clipboard. My stomach somersaulted at the sight of it and I looked away.

She turned to me and I realized I had missed whatever exchange took place on the buzzer intercom.

"I'm going to go see him," she said.

I realized my work was done, that I was no longer needed, and she was now flinging me aside.

I smiled because it was the easiest way to say nothing.

The door buzzed, and she pulled the handle. I watched her walk away from me through the glass door.

"Do you believe in gay rights?"

I turned to find the flag too close to me, the clipboard imposing itself in my space.

"What?"

"We're obtaining signatures to petition for gay rights. Not just on campus. Everywhere. We want to send this to Washington."

I was at a loss for words and yet I felt the sweat as it cooled between my shoulder blades and upon the back of my neck.

"I'm not gay."

He stared at me with his head slightly bent to the side. His mouth was half open and the ever so short spikes of his dirty blonde hair glistened as rain fell upon him. I marveled at how pink his lips were, how translucently blue his eyes.

"I didn't ask if you were gay. I asked if you believed in gay rights."

"I believe in all rights," I said.

"Great. Then will you sign the petition?"

"No," I said as I brushed past him.

His clipboard clattered as it hit the pavement.

I didn't want to look back at him but I did. I felt my face getting hotter and redder as I watched him silently bend to pick up his clipboard and the pen that had rolled away. He still held onto the stick with the rainbow.

As my pace quickened to a jog, I felt the moisture upon my face, my cheeks, my chin. It wasn't the rain that made me uneasy. It was the tears that were streaming with the rainwater, signaling something very wrong had happened that afternoon.

Chapter Nine

"I can't see," said the man across from me. He had huge nostrils and was blowing air through them as does a bull.

"Put them on, sir." I said as politely as I could.

"I don't need a two dollar an hour employee telling me what to do."

I swallowed. I waited for the wave of anger to wash over me. It didn't. Basically, the anger came in a wave and submerged me and I stayed under trying very desperately to breathe.

"I want my money back."

I met his black eyes.

"There are no refunds, sir. And you haven't even tried them on."

"I did."

"For 20 seconds. Please put them on."

"Everything is blurry when I put them on."

He sat back in his chair and crossed his hairy arms. I could feel Ed's chuckle from across the room. It wasn't that Ed wouldn't help me in difficult situations, but this didn't qualify. Difficult was someone rising from the chair, gesturing, using profanity and seeming threatening. It would seem that no one would do that at a doctor's practice, but they did more often than I could remember. Maybe it was something about eyeglasses that made people vulnerable.

"Sir, they are reading glasses. If you look out at the distance, everything will be blurry."

He uncrossed his massive arms and placed two tiny, sweaty hands on the table, the palms flat, the fingers slightly curled.

"What? What kind of shit is that?"

"Well, sir, you have a problem with reading, not distance. So, they are reading glasses. If you put them on and read the card I tried to hand you, you will see the print clearly. That's what we're trying to do."

He kept his gaze fixed at my face. His hands remained unmoved. I held out the glasses and waited. Finally, he took them with a snatch, put them on and took the reading card from the table.

"Holy shit, you don't say."

I heard him mumble as he read the print about Ben Franklin inventing bifocals. I knew by heart by now how Ben had come up with the ingenious idea and waited patiently for the big, hairy man to finish mumbling. He eventually did and slowly removed the glasses.

"These are fucking amazing. I can read the small stuff."

He gestured to the very bottom of the card.

"I can read that."

"I'm happy you're happy." I said.

"I need a case and one of those cloth things."

I handed him a green fake leatherette case with 20/20 emblazoned in gold. It was open and inside, there was a cloth to match the case, also with 20/20 written across it but silkscreened in black. He took the case, placed the glasses inside and rose to leave. He left abruptly as if I had taken up too much of his afternoon.

"Thank you!" I screamed as the door closed behind him and the bells jangled wildly.

"A fucking 'thank you' would have been nice, asshole."

"Now, now easy there, kiddo," Ed said as he tried not to laugh.

"Ed why do we do this anyway? I mean as a job. There are a million jobs in the world."

"You fall into it. I can't explain how, but it's a weird thing. No one ever grows up saying 'I want to be an optician.' You fall into it. But Priya, the lives and the stories opticians can tell you. Great stuff for your writing."

"You won't tell me yours."

Ed took in a breath and held it as he tried to think of the words to say. I almost regretted my statement. He scratched his chin and I pondered how Ed would look with a goatee. He was a handsome man overall even if he was over sixty. A goatee might make him more dignified than goofy. I was sure of that. His brown and white hair would sit well in a goatee and hide his winsome smile making him appear more mysterious.

"Ed, I didn't mean—"

He smiled slightly.

"I'll tell you someday," he said.

"Will you?"

"I promise."

"Why?"

"Because, Priya, she was one hell of a woman. And ours was one hell of a story."

Chapter Ten

"It's a great story," she said as she looked up from the paper. I was concentrating on the page in front of her, my handwriting uneven and strong in blue against the white, ink showing through to the other side. She held 20 pages or so and was on the last one, the one half-written as the story had ended at that.

I wanted her to say more, to tell me how I had touched her heart.

"Do you like it?" was all I could think of to solicit what I wanted to hear.

"I love it."

I heard "I love" in her voice and wanted the next word to be "you."

I had waited almost a year of knowing her before I showed her my writing. I never told her I wrote, that since I had seen her, known her, I closed my eyes and envisioned her essence before bringing it onto paper. But I wanted to share it with her after a realization that we shared a friendship but not intimacies. Although intimacy, I learned, is mutual, not a one-sided dance that has any beauty of its own; it needs a partner.

She had just told me he had kissed her, that he had held her hand after. So, I offered her a short story I had written thinking it would erase from her mind the physical intimacy she had shared with him and somehow leave her beholden to me. Nothing of the sort happened. She read the story, made a sound in her throat here and there while reading, and handed it back to me with "I love it."

"Would you like some lunch?" she asked.

"No."

"Aren't you hungry? It's almost three o'clock."

"Not hungry."

I felt bruised. And I knew I was being short with her just for her to ask what was wrong, for a drop of concern to swim across her beautiful eyes. But I also knew that I didn't know what was wrong, just that the more I knew her, the more I wanted, the less I learned to expect, the more restless I became. Sometimes I wondered if I should not know her, if perhaps this acquaintance would leave me emptier than the emptiness of not having her fill the spaces of my mind and soul. But then, but then she would smile as she did now, shake off any affront I may or may not have delivered and graze my hand with her fingertips.

"You're grumpy because you're hungry," she said.

"No."

"But yes. Yes, my love, yes. Let's get you something to eat. My treat."

My love. My love. My love.

Chapter Eleven

The rain was hard and the wind was relentless. I pulled my jacket closer to myself and wondered how August could be so harsh. Ordinarily, I would have been sleeping in warm sheets with the air conditioner blasting but Sam had insisted I meet with him at seven in the morning and had promised me a day off later in the week. For anyone else, I probably would not have ventured out and would have insisted that a day off means a day off. But my proximity to work and Sam's pleading tone made me feel guilty for refusing. He had said something about talking about the "fate of the business" and, although I knew him to be melodramatic most times about 20/20, I always wondered when he spoke like this if this was the one time it was indeed melodrama and not just his exaggeration of a simple problem or, as was more often than not, his concern of making even more money.

When Sam had taken 20/20, it was a humble business boasting close to $100,000 in sales. In the three years we had worked together, we had turned that humble number into a proud and cool quarter million. It was Sam's foresight, my tenaciousness, Ed's skill, and the doctor's good moods and graces that had allowed us to function, however dysfunctional we were, to achieving those numbers.

If Ed had said that every optician had a story, Sam's was no less compelling. He had graduated high school at the bottom of his class, chased a pretty woman to Las Vegas, managed a casino under her father's supervision, been dumped, jobless, and hopeless, and worked as a security guard to pay for a room with three other guys and to put himself through optical school. Just when he seemed fated to be a cranky, disgruntled optician, his father had died and left him sums of money that he used to buy a run-down optical, turn it around, sell it, and then invest in 20/20 which, for some reason, had become the motive and love of his life.

As I turned the corner to reach work, I saw Sam pacing outside the store umbrella-less, the store gate up, door I was sure unlocked.

When I reached him, he stopped to look at me, his eyes bloodshot yet alert.

"Sam why are you pacing outside in the rain? Are you crazy?"

"Waiting for you."

"You could have waited inside."

He shrugged and pushed the door open for us, the bells clanging as we entered. He locked the door and while I thought we would head to his office, he took a seat in a patient's chair at the front selling station. I took off my jacket and hung it on the chair across from him, threw my umbrella to the floor, and sat down.

"Sam, are you okay?"

"I'm firing her today. I haven't slept all night. Not that I feel guilty. I mean she's terrible. But I feel bad. Like I'm blindsiding her. But the new doctor, I slated her to start in two weeks. I can't wait anymore. Exams are down. She leaves early. Comes in whenever she wants."

"You're firing Dr. Bello today?" I asked with a disbelief that I realized instead of assuaging was sure to compound his guilt.

"Yes, Priya. That's why you're here."

I looked at his eyes and he averted his gaze and concentrated on the frames behind me.

"That's why *I'm* here? You think *I'm* going to do it?"

"No, no. But you'll be with me. I need you with me. I can't do this alone. She'll be here at eight. I told her to come in early to discuss financials."

I looked at his jacket which he hadn't removed and watched the rainwater seeping into the fabric of the chair.

"Take your jacket off." I said. "You're wetting the chair."

"See, Priya, that's why I need you." He said as he wriggled out of the jacket and flung it over the back of the chair. "You think of everything. And I can't be alone with that woman when I'm telling her she has two weeks."

"Sam, you're a big boy."

"She scares me, Priya."

I couldn't help but laugh and this made Sam laugh also. His was a boyish laugh and it brought out his features, the glow in his warm brown albeit bloodshot eyes.

"So tell me about our new doctor. Will I like her."

"You'll love her, Priya. When I was in school and I took a class in business, the professor said to us, 'Don't find a doctor to hire for your practice; find someone to love.' Priya, she's someone to love."

"What is so special about this doctor?"

"What is so special? Besides the fact that she

57

graduated top of her class at SUNY? That she spent summers traveling and providing exams in countries like Guatemala and India and Brazil without a clinic, without much more than trial lenses and an ophthalmoscope and enjoyed doing it? That she's charming and took the first offer I made which is 15 percent less than Bello is milking me for? What's so special?"

"Sounds like a poster child for optometry."

Sam leaned in and rest his forearms on the table. I thought he was about to tell me a great secret, the way he arched his body and locked eyes with me.

"Truth is, Priya, everything I just said is true. But it's more than that. You'll see when you meet her. This woman just makes you feel, I don't know, safe. Like you can trust her. And like she's genuine."

"Are you in love, Sam?" I joked.

"Priya my first and last love is 20/20. You know this."

"Sadly, my friend, I do. Why haven't I met her, by the way?"

"How, Priya? If I invite her here, Bello will be suspicious. And if I invite her out somewhere, she'll be suspicious."

"I'm going to make some coffee," Sam said as he rose from his chair and headed to his office to fire up the Keurig.

"What's her name?" I asked.

He turned and smiled as if just saying her name made him happy.

"Dr. L.M. Ibrahim."

"Do you have a crush, Sam?"

"Yes, Priya, a crush on 20/20 and a very bright future for us. Listen, join me for some coffee. I think I have some cookies back there too. And when Bello comes in, we'll tackle this together."

"I don't want your stale, moldy cookies," I said as I followed him.

"Well that's all I got. Listen, since you're here anyway, can't you just work the day later this week? I'll pay you out."

"Pay me out? You said I could take off later this week."

He stopped walking and turned to me, placing warm hands on my shoulders.

"Priya, how can I run this place without you? I mean I'll pay you time and a half for today. Promise. Just do it. Please. When it's just Ed, it's disastrous. He's a great guy but the charm with which *you* sell... please."

"Fine. I have no life anyway."

He gently gave my shoulders a squeeze.

"Thanks. Glad to know you're in the 'no life opticians' club."

We went to the office and silently drank coffee, waiting for Dr. Bello to arrive.

Chapter Twelve

I used to travel to Calcutta in the summers when I was younger, during that blazing, scorching heat when no one sane would ever choose to travel to Calcutta. But our relief was the monsoons, dark and ominous yet cool, a break to the monotony of heat and desperation. It was where I spent summer vacations and never was it a vacation but a spilling over from one life to the next, my dualities never reconciling, even now when I thought about them.

I never had the sprawling and large families that people complained about openly in a secret boast. I had two aunts on my mother's side and my father's ailing parents to visit. No siblings. And one cousin. Or should I say I had one cousin. And that was him.

Whether someone or something becomes more precious when it is not a commodity but a uniqueness or whether I adored him because he was the only brother I knew, I don't know. I think again about the rope he used to sever his ties with the world and wonder as to its thickness, its weight, its feel upon his slender neck.

I tied rakhee on his wrist for the last time three years ago, on a hiatus from jobs, before 20/20 when, in a frustrated and righteous rage declared my visits to

Calcutta were going to occur when I wanted them to and I was not bound to a covenant that said every year I had to see only one hemisphere of the world and forsake all others. I wanted to travel the world, not perch on a familiar peninsula every chance that I had.

Chance had everything to do with it or maybe it was foreshadowing that I see now, in hindsight. I had just tied the rakhee on his wrist, the tinsel not shining but wilting with the weight of the om decoration that was embedded in the center. I anointed his forehead with vermillion, sandalwood paste, rice, wished him a good and long and happy life. And then, when I raised the plate with the diya that stay lit with its dancing flame, the flame flickered. Before my mother or his could run over and cup a hand over the flame to revive it, there was no flame but smoke and the memory of where a flame had once been.

Unease permeated the air and then their voices chiding me as if I had willed ill will upon the entire ceremony, informing me of the misfortune that would follow with the extinguishing of a flame.

I did not shrug it off then and I never have. Every time I spoke to him or of him thereafter until I no longer could because he willingly traversed from life to into death, I waited and the feeling of anticipating misfortune lingered. I wondered now for the first time since July, since I heard of his demise, if that morning, if that failed attempt at a blessing had cursed him from that precise moment and if I had been the one to take his life in a circuitous course of fate.

"Fate is written in the stars," she said.

We were gazing at a dark sky somewhere up in Vermont, an astronomy excursion that we had both

61

enrolled for. The stars were large and heavy and remained suspended in a dark velvet sky.

"You believe in such things?" I asked.

"I do. You have to believe in something or you'll just float away."

"Do you believe in God?" I asked as I adjusted the palms of my hands under my head on the blanket and watched her adjust the telescope.

"Yes," she said so faintly that I almost didn't hear. She lowered the telescope and then turned and in one motion dropped onto the blanket and lay next to me. I thanked her stars, her God for such a mercy, for the peace, for the one moment in so many lost moments of life that I closed my eyes and was genuinely content and happy, her breathing a shallow river next to my ear.

"Do you?" she asked softly.

My mind slipped from the euphoria of stars and the tickle of her hair on my arm to wanting more than I should have, more than what would ever be granted to me in this life and instead of the gratitude that had flickered a moment ago I found a flame of fury inside myself for not being able to turn and lie on her shoulder or graze her fingers with my knuckles. Greed is great disillusionment and I was greedy wanting more than a vast expanse of Universe with her lying at my side. I wanted the stars to burst and shower desire and passion into the vast expanse of our souls, to be able to forget that I could not touch her or even seem as if I wanted to. And all of a sudden the word fell like a cursed and broken shooting star:

"No."

Looking back, I wondered how I had constructed

62

a world of us, of her and me, how I had allowed an "us" at all. Looking back, I wondered if I had shattered that world with my ingratitude and insolence, denying the presence of a God when clearly, he was holding us uplifted from the rest of the Universe at that precise moment, allowing her to lie next to me on a grassy hill in Vermont while stars shone with messages of fate. How could I have denied God at the moment when he shone brightest?

I was the gust of wind that extinguished flames, that held foreboding and evil fates at the tips of my fingers, somewhere deep in my throat.

"You will," she said. "Someday you will."

Did I believe now? With her gone 17 years and him dead, craving for their voices or an intonation of laughter that I would never again hear, did I now believe in her God?

I believed in blessings and curses, in unspoken messages spoken through extinguished flames and falling stars. I believed most of all that I was the curse that delivered their fates. Presumptuous maybe but at least I wasn't blaming a God for all that went wrong in our lives.

But she had been right about one thing as she had been about so much else: they had at least moved to different things (her I didn't know to what, him to death) whereas I was floating through life hoping for an anchor.

Chapter Thirteen

Dr. Bello entered 20/20 bringing with her a gust of rainwater. She let the door go and it clanged violently behind her. I looked at the clock on the wall above the dispensing counter and saw that it was 8:25. I looked at Sam who was sitting in one of the chairs by the doctor's office, arms crossed, waiting patiently with obvious impatience.

"Sam, this better be good," Dr. Bello said. "I am not paid to arrive an hour and a half early in the middle of a tsunami."

"It's good," Sam countered.

He waited for her to walk past him and into her office where we both heard her set down her enormous Louis Vuitton. There were random sounds and I heard, above all of them, Sam's deepening breaths as he remained calm with much effort. He rose and walked to me and sat across from me at the selling station.

"Just today. And then two weeks. And then that's it."

"Sam, take it easy."

"I don't even know why I gave her two weeks. I didn't have to."

"Because you're fair. And good. That's why."

Dr. Bello walked out of her office, her fingers in

her hair, loosening the blonde curls that ended a little past her neck. She stopped and stood, waiting.

"Dr. Bello let's all go to my office," Sam suggested.

"We can talk out here, Sam. There's no one here. And your office smells like coffee."

"Very well. Have a seat."

Sam motioned for the selling station adjacent to where he and I sat. Dr. Bello reluctantly turned a chair towards us and took a seat. The apprehension was palpable, and I wished for a moment I was not there.

"Dr. Bello, do you know why I called you in today?" Sam began.

"No, Sam, I do not. All I know is I woke up at five to be here an hour and a half early through a torrential rainstorm. So, why don't you tell me?"

Sam made a steeple with his fingertips.

"Dr. Bello, the key to any business, especially ours, is patient care. Patient care is achieved through consistency."

I looked at Dr. Bellow askance and she wore a slight pout.

"Well, Sam, I'm glad you brought that up. Thing is, you take care of me and I take care of the patients. As it is, I've been trying to get you to see that what you pay me is not enough for all that you have me do."

Sam sighed a deep, long sigh. I saw him look directly into her eyes and my body clenched.

"Dr. Bello, I'm not here to offer you a raise. I am here to, in fact, tell you that after the next two weeks, your services will no longer be needed at 20/20."

The silence that followed was taut.

Dr. Bello rose from her chair.

"How dare you! After everything I have done for you and this stupid place. You can't just kick me out the door, Sam. There are laws."

"There are no laws that require me to keep paying you an astronomical salary to do what someone else will do for less. There are no laws that state that you can come and go as you please and I have to tolerate your schedule."

I saw Sam turning red, his brown eyes gleaming as if he had practiced and waited to deliver this dialogue for a long time.

"Sam, I will not be talked to that way. You know what? Forget the two weeks, Sam. Forget your charity of a fortnight. I quit now! I leave now. And to hell with 20/20."

Sam looked as if he had been slapped. He rose from his chair and stood across from her. They faced each other and did nothing but stare and breathe hard.

"You think you'll find someone better than me? You think you won't suffer for months without my credentials, without my patients?"

"They are not *your* patients. They are 20/20's patients."

Dr. Bello took a step towards him. I shot up from the chair.

"Guys, there must be a better way than this. Let's sit down and talk this through."

They turned to me as if they had forgotten I was in the room.

"There is no better way, Priya," Dr. Bello said.

She walked past Sam and her heels made an uneven rhythm as she walked to her office. Sam looked at the ceiling. I looked at Sam. We both heard her open and slam drawers, scuttling across her office floor and then back. The time seemed to pass slowly as if trapped in an hourglass of tension.

When she emerged, Dr. Bello's Louis Vuitton was stuffed. She held in her hands a plastic bag filled with dress shoes and her white doctor's coat.

"You ingrate!" she screamed. "After everything I have done to make you a rich man."

"I made you rich too. Don't you forget that!"

It felt more like a lover's quarrel than a termination. I watched as she took dignified, determined steps and reached the door. She paused. She said nothing. Then she flung the door wide, let herself through, and let it slam with a heavy jangle. She was gone.

"What are we going to do for two weeks?" I finally said.

Sam came behind me and rested his heavy palms on my shoulders. The weight was comforting, as if he were holding me down so I wouldn't float away.

"I don't know, Priya. Pray, I guess."

I turned to face him and although he wore a faint smile, I saw in his eyes the worry I felt within myself. 20/20 hadn't been without a doctor, without Dr. Bello, since we had opened our doors.

"It'll be okay, Sam."

"Of course, it will," he said with false optimism. Then, "all we need to do is have a little faith."

Chapter Fourteen

"We just have to have faith that everything is for the best," she said.

Outside, the sky was gray and pregnant with a threat of great rain. Inside her dorm room, we were lying on an extra-long twin bed, not as lovers but as devastated friends.

She reached for my hand and I allowed her to take it. She placed it on her abdomen and pressed slightly.

"For this would have been where my baby grew," she said.

I think back to the last 36 hours, her frantic call, my rushing over despite being in the middle of a philosophy test, the blood staining her skirt, the hospital. Although she hadn't decided to carry a life inside herself, it had happened of its own accord. And she hadn't told me. And I hadn't known. It was too soon for the telltale signs. Even when she called, she did not say, "I am losing my child." All I heard was her uneven and jagged breath, her fear caught within her throat. When I arrived, I saw the blood on her skirt, her pacing back and forth saying "Oh, my God. Oh, my God."

I accompanied her to the student medical center and then the hospital and the rise of resentment that rose to flush my cheeks embarrassed me. But was he not supposed to make an appearance? Was he not as responsible or as concerned as she about *their* child? I wanted to hurl questions at her with a scream but instead whispered softly, "Does he know?"

"He knows," she said.

"Then where is he?"

"He is away with friends. He doesn't know I lost it. I called you. I didn't call him."

I waited with her the night and then part of the morning at the hospital. When we arrived back to her dorm, she asked me to stay.

And while we lay on her bed, while my hand was on her stomach, she said, "I wish he were here."

I had perhaps never felt as useless, as much of a proxy than I did at that moment. Why was I not enough? Why was the weight and heat of my hand upon her not enough to calm and soothe her and make her content?

"What would he do?" I asked, trying not to let hurt tinge my voice.

"He would just make everything better."

I felt the pull he had on her, what I am sure is called love. But I was there. Why couldn't I make everything better? Why was I not making everything better?

"You wanted to have a child?" I asked. And then, "with him?"

She turned to me and I saw the tears slipping from the corners of her eyes.

"I didn't plan to have a child. But once it happened, I wanted to have a child. It would have changed everything. I know that. But I was willing for that change. I love him, Priya. And I would have loved our child as well."

I tried to swallow her words, but they lodged somewhere in my throat and I couldn't speak.

"I thought once, at the very beginning, when I found out, about not having it. But that thought left as quickly as it came. But I wonder now if that's the thought the Universe heard and felt, if that's why I lost it. If it's somehow… "

She stopped talking and I, despite the jealousy and confusion stuck in my throat, forced myself to speak.

"Somehow what?"

"Somehow my fault."

"This is not your fault," I said as my eyes caught her bloody skirt flung over the back of her chair. I allowed my hand to move to her face and my fingertips to wipe her tears although they kept spilling into the gray afternoon as if the rains were falling not from the sky but from her eyes.

"I wish none of it had happened," she said. And then, slowly and softly, "I wish he had wanted our child more. He didn't say he didn't. But he never said he did."

With that she turned away from me, pulled my arm across her, laced her fingers through mine, and was silent.

I wished I were him and I could show her happiness. As myself, I could not because my words, my actions, my body were not enough. Although I knew that if we were stripped of everything but our souls, she would see that mine would jump with magnetism towards her just as his would. Except if I could enter the places in her that he so easily inhabited, her heart, her mind, her desire, I would also allow her to occupy me. He might have loved her, but he was not consumed with her. And that saddened me.

I didn't know enough of love then (and I don't believe I do now) but I envisioned it as a geode of colors, jagged and mixed with hurt and pain. That's what I did know of love, that she loved him beyond reason and was saddened by it, that he loved her and yet was not completely beholden to her essence.

I didn't know what I called it but she was in my thoughts and infused into my very being. I wanted her to look at me, to talk about me as she did him. The mere thought filled me with unease, washed me with shame although I didn't know why or whence this shame arrived or decided to nestle into me. I tried to extricate my hand from hers for the simple touch was not so simple. And although I thought her asleep, her grip tightened, and she spoke.

"Priya?"

I jumped slightly within myself as if she could read my thoughts. As if she were going to comment, tell me how wrong and how perverted my conscience was. Or perhaps my shame would speak of its own accord and admit the trajectories of my own thoughts and confusion.

"You need something?" I asked.

"Just don't let go."

"I won't," I said. "I won't."

Chapter Fifteen

"I won't." He said. "I won't. I won't. I won't."

We were on the terrace, he and I, sitting cross legged, facing each other on a thatched mat with a woven pink border. We were playing House Full with a pack of faded and creased cards that, instead of kings and queens and jacks and numbers had Campa Cola bottles in various colors and flavors. The goal was to get four cards of the same cola drink. I had three Campa Oranges and picked up a Lemon card only to discard it onto the messy pile between us.

"So then tell them." I said.

He shook his head side to side, picked up the lemon card and then placed a card face down on the messy pile.

"Campa Lemon" he said as he splayed four lemon cards onto the mat.

I threw my cards onto the mat as well.

"I'm not marrying her, Priya," he said.

"Then just tell them that."

He brought his knees up to his chest and put his arms around his thin shins.

"If not her then someone else. They don't stop, Priya."

"So what do you want?" I asked.

"To be free."

He rose in one quick motion and walked the length of the terrace until he was at the edge. He looked down at the city, the haze of heat and smoke catching in the air.

"So, what are you going to do?" I asked.

"I don't know." And then, "I will meet her."

"Why?"

"Because."

"Because?"

"Because meeting and rejecting someone is easier than just rejecting the idea of someone. I can play this game too."

"This is not a game, Prem."

"They have made it so."

He turned to me. He took my hands in his and looked into me with empty eyes.

"Help me through this, please."

Unable to speak all of a sudden, I simply nodded in agreement.

Chapter Sixteen

Both Sam and I had thought that having no doctor on premises would hinder business but, surprisingly, we were doing quite well in the absence of Dr. Bello. Part of the reason was that Ed, however goofy and somewhat lazy as he was, had made rounds to some ophthalmology offices that had no dispensaries and had deposited 20/20 cards with their receptionists. Although this seemed like a long shot, we were getting those same patients to walk in with prescriptions and we were selling just slightly less than when we had a doctor.

"This is luck, kiddo," Ed said as he closed an eye to thread a nylon string through the tiny hole in the metal of a semi-rimless.

"I know, Ed but thank God for this, at least."

"We need this doctor sooner rather than later. What do we know about her anyway?"

I watched Ed poke at the hole and miss, poke again and have the string not thread through. Without a word I took the frame and nylon from him not because I was in any was any more adept but because my eyes were younger and I could focus better at a close distance even if he were wearing his progressives. I threaded the nylon and tried handing the frame back to Ed. He put his hands up in the air as if in surrender and smiled.

"No, no. You took it, you finish it," he said mockingly.

I busied myself with the frame and nylon string.

"Her name is L.M. Ibrahim," I offered since this is all that I really knew anyway.

"How long has she been practicing?"

"I don't know but she's been to all these countries performing free exams with trial lenses and an ophthalmoscope."

Ed sighed as if in deep thought.

"That tells me absolutely nothing," he said.

"How bad could she be?" I asked. "I mean she's looking at eyeballs all day. One or two. Red or green. How bad could she really fuck that up?"

"Watch your fucking language," Ed said jokingly and started laughing at his own humor.

"Ed, I'm serious." I said. "I mean how bad could she really be?"

"Not bad at all, kiddo but we have to stare at her for eight to 10 hours a day. I hope she's pleasant at least. Or pretty. I hope she's pretty so it'll make the staring worthwhile."

"Yes, Ed." I said. "I am sure that was Sam's criteria. Forget SUNY and forget her charity eye exams abroad, we hope she is pretty for you to stare at."

"Precisely," Ed said as if in all seriousness and then slowly started examining the trays by the lensometer as if just looking down at them would get the inspection done itself.

"Ed, check jobs, will you? We have so many there and all these people are calling to see if their glasses are ready."

"I'm living the dream," Ed said as he placed a pair of glasses in the lensometer and clamped the lens stop down.

I fiddled with the nylon making sure the lens was tight and then threaded it through the final hole and cut the string. I sprayed the lenses with some cleaner, wiped and set the glasses aside in a tray marked "Repair. Holtz" followed by a phone number. I would call later. I leaned an elbow on the counter and watched Ed stare into the lensometer with one eye, his other eye suspended in a permanent wink as his hands moving simultaneously on the axis wheel and power drum, checking, pulling up the lens stop, placing the other lens under scrutiny, checking again. I loved watching him work because he was so adept, so fast and it was so juxtaposed to my gentle and calculated turning of wheels and slight guesstimations.

"What, you're just going to watch me?"

"What else would you have me do?"

Ed grunted and went back to the lenspiece. We heard the door jangle and turned together to watch a woman walk in followed by five children ranging in age from about four to 11. They reminded me of ducks crossing the street.

"We need glasses," the woman stated.

"Sure," I said as Ed turned back to the lensometer.

"When can I have them?" she asked.

"May I see the prescriptions?" I asked.

"Oh, just one, just for John," she said as she pushed the youngest and smallest child to me as if surrendering him.

The other children seemed to disperse around the counters smashing greasy fingers into the glass at various frames and sunglasses. I tried to ignore them and stared hard at John's prescription.

"Well, these are going to have to be ordered," I said. "It seems he has a high prescription. Is it for strabismus?"

"Stra who?"

"Um, sorry. Lazy eye?"

I looked up and she frowned.

"That's what the doctor said. I think it's the video games and computer. The tablet. They all have tablets you know. My husband would rather them be quiet than have good vision."

"Let's see what we can find," I said all the while ignoring her comments. It's an art really to be able to ignore comments. The natural inclination, as in any form of defense against stupidity, is to react, to offer a rebuttal. But over time in optical, I learned the best defense was always silence because, most times, it didn't warrant more comments but a sweet return of silence or at least a change of topic.

The only way I could get John to try on frames was to pretend he was shooting me with a toy frog he held and pretended to aim. It was only after an "Ow, you got me," or "Woah! Good shot!" that he would even allow a frame to be slipped onto his ears and nose. The problem was, John was very small with a shallow bridge and most of the frames slid right off him. It was a lazy afternoon and an annoying one as I saw the frames pile up on the counter, then watched the other children grab them and try them on themselves and, intermittently, when she remembered, heard the mother tell the children quite disinterestedly not to touch anything although they were running around with frames and giggling.

Finally, after what was an excruciating 45 minutes or so we found John a metal, electric blue frame and a matte black one from the same collection in the same size. I hastily wrote the tickets. Now came time for the pupillary distance and I squirmed.

"John, I need you to look at me," I said as I held the pupilometer in my hand.

"What's that?"

"It's just to take a measurement," I tried.

"No!" John retorted as he hugged tight his mother's thigh.

"John—" I started again.

"No."

I lay the pupilometer on the counter and rubbed my temples. I was thinking of what to do when I heard Ed bellow from behind me.

"Come here, fella," he said.

With that, he bent down, pulled a ruler from his shirt pocket and laid it across John's shallow bridge.

"That's it," Ed said with a smile. Then, turning to me, "Fifty."

He walked back to the lensometer and turned his back to us as he started checking jobs again.

With that, I collected payment. After placing her credit card gingerly back in her wallet, the mother pried frames from all the children except John who was not interested in frames but in shooting Ed with his toy frog. When all the frames were placed on the counter and there were disappointed and confused shouts from the children, the mother commanded that they follow her and I watched the ducks file out, the mother first followed by a gaggle of screaming children. The door shut, jangled, and then all was silent once again.

"Thanks, Ed."

"You want to thank me, kiddo?"

"I just did," I said puzzled.

Ed turned away from the counter and gave me his signature goofy smile.

"So you check jobs and let me go get a snack," he said as he stepped towards the door. Before I could answer he had left and I stood there nodding, loving and being annoyed with him at the same time. I turned to the counter and started checking the pair of glasses still suspended in the lensometer. He had been so eager to get his snack that he hadn't even finished the pair he had been inspecting. I looked through the eyepiece and knew I should calibrate the entire thing but didn't. I wondered if Ed's laziness was rubbing off on me or if I were just becoming jaded and bored.

When Ed returned, he handed me an ice cream cone with sprinkles although I never quite liked sprinkles, something about the texture making them seem like pieces of plastic in my mouth.

"Now we both can't inspect jobs," he said cheerily as he licked his swirled chocolate and vanilla soft serve.

"Authentic Mr. Softie, Priya," he said. "Right on the corner."

"Gourmet," I said as I took a lick of soft serve myself.

When Sam walked in, he saw Ed and me behind the counter licking soft serve cones, the counter a mess of trays, a pair of glasses half-inspected and suspended in the lensometer. Such was life at 20/20.

Chapter Seventeen

Bhoot pisach nikat nahin ave / Mahavir jab naam sunave

No ghost dare come / When one utters the name of the brave one

It was Tuesday night, the night after the gaggle of children, and, although I should have read the *Chalisa* upon waking, I found it most peaceful and liberating to recite the verses in the evening after returning from work and showering. That night also I was halfway through, stopping and loving each line for more reasons than I knew when I heard my phone chime with some Bollywood song again and again. When I stared at the screen I saw it was my parents and my stomach clenched. I continued reciting and tried to ignore the call.

It wasn't that I didn't want to speak to them. It was more that I knew they would offer more information about his death, the cremation, the ultimate releasing of ashes into a sacred river. It was more that they would insist that while everyone knew how and approximately when, no one knew *why* he had chosen such, as they called it, "a drastic measure." They insisted he could have talked to someone although to whom they never said, and I don't believe they knew.

After I finished reciting the 40 verses, I closed my eyes and all I could see were his eyes, his solemn face full of some misery only he understood. And as I stood there, trying to pray, I wondered why no one else ever saw that misery. They referred to him even now as quiet but happy and content and I wondered wherein there was the lie, in his soulful eyes or in their hollow words.

After I finished false prayers (because there was nothing real about praying for peace and happiness when all I could think of was a young man's suicide and all that rose within me was anger and turmoil and there was nothing real about decrying that no ghosts come near with His name when the ghosts of the past were embedded deep into my own soul) I sat on the rim of the tub and lit a cigarette. What were his last, his very last thoughts, I wondered? And were there words? Did he say anything that was absorbed as vibration into the air around him not to be heard by a single soul? Were his eyes still tainted with want and misery?

As I exhaled, I remember the misery her eyes had held once. I closed my eyes and was taken back to a small Chinese restaurant, streamers and balloons decorating the establishment, 20 or so of us collected to wish her a happy birthday and offer presents, one hoping to outdo the other. But her eyes were far, and her thoughts were farther.

It was only two weeks after we were lying in an extra-long twin bed, her whispering and crying and me consoling the loss of a child, her child. He hadn't spoken to her since then, even upon his return from wherever he had gone with friends. She had tried calling only to have his roommate huff that he wasn't there although she knew he must have been or at least believed so. When she called him directly, his phone was not ever on and she left a solitary voicemail message simply asking him to call her, but he never did.

We shut the restaurant lights off amid much protest from the owner couple who argued that people would think they were closed. We argued that it would take five minutes to cut a cake and the 20 of us were bringing in more money than anyone else would that evening. In the dark, I lit 21 candles, one for good luck and all, and carried out the cake, a monstrous rectangle with chocolate mousse icing and three layers of deep rich chocolate sponge cake.

I set the cake down in front of her and as the "happy birthday" song escalated in mismatched voices and various pitches, I happened to glance into her eyes and they carried such weight and misery I couldn't look away. With a gaze, she was saying, "Don't let me go." Except this time, I knew she wished to say this to him, not to me and I could do nothing to bring him back. I could not deliver to her happiness and above anything that I felt that befuddled me or left me answerless, this inability to make her happy as they sang happy birthday seemed the biggest and saddest oxymoron of all.

When she blew out the candles, a spray of liquid paraffin landed on the collar of my shirt and hardened into a deep red. She closed her eyes, made a wish, and then opened them again. She cut the cake, there was laughter and clapping, and then the lights were switched on again. My eyes smarted with the infusion of light. When I looked at her, she was smiling and yet her eyes were still not. I gently grazed her cheek with a half open fist, my knuckles teasing her soft skin. I was unaware that I did this but did it to impart some understanding, some affection when she seemed to lack it most. She looked at me and smiled, winked suddenly as if to say, "all is well" when we both knew it wasn't and then turned to continue half hanging conversations.

As she spoke to random people about random things, I heard a whisper I wished I had not heard. It was behind my left shoulder, I remember, at the seat of the devil.

"Where's her boyfriend?" was a voice.

"I don't know but Priya's doing a damn good job of filling in." Voice Two.

"Is she her best friend or is she *in love with* Leyla?" Voice One.

"You mean you can't tell? She's obsessed. But the funny thing is, Leyla leads her on. And I think, I think she doesn't even have a clue." Voice Two.

Two voices. Two streams of laughter. That's all it took for me to unravel from her. Not in a generic way or in a way that was simple. It was not an unwinding but a volcanic destruction of her. Of us. After which there would be no Voice One. No Voice Two. No speculation. No rumors.

Did what followed happen with intention? Of course not. But hindsight is a blessing as much as it is a curse. And if I looked back now I perhaps could see the desperation in what followed, at least from my part. It was a desperate plea, after all was said and done, to be young and accepted and a part of something. To be unclothed by two whispers, to be exposed to myself of being and feeling what I tried most to deny led to the spiral that occurred. I knew that sitting on the rim of a tub, smoke swirling around me in madness. But back then, for whatever transpired, all I believed was that I was the bad thing that happened to good people.

Chapter Eighteen

"I am the bad thing that happens to good people," he said.

It was night time and the song of the crickets was rhythmic and loud. A single bulb hung from the ceiling casting a yellow orange glow. We were in the small room reserved for prayers because everyone was asleep and there was nowhere to sit in the small apartment save the terrace and the room of prayers, a makeshift temple and altar of sorts.

"Why do you say that?" I asked.

He turned to me, his chin resting on his knees, his arms encircling his shins. He was rocking slightly back and forth. His eyes looked up at me and he looked more like a lost boy than a man.

He sighed. He closed his eyes.

"I feel bad for Aasthika."

"What's the matter, Prem? What happened?"

Here he held his breath.

I remember the heat of the night, the scent of extinguished queen of the night incense enveloping us. And a hint of camphor in the air. I looked from him to the statues of idols, to the walls adorned with posters of more idols. I looked from Kali to Durga to Shiva and then rest my eyes on a three foot idol of Hanuman. A stray cockroach scuttled across the floor.

"I said 'yes,'" he said.

"Yes to what?"

"To marrying her."

I rose from the floor. I paced a haphazard circle around the small room, nearly falling twice.

"Are you mad? Have you gone insane?" I asked.

He shrugged and placed his head between his knees. When he spoke, the sound was muffled.

"It just happened."

"It just happened? It just happened? How does something like that just happen?"

He tried to relay the story to me. Yet no matter what he said or how he said it, I didn't understand his acquiescence. And I don't think he did either.

"They came for tea, remember?"

"Yes, they did."

He picked his head up and looked up at me. I didn't hold his gaze but keep forming jagged circles around the room.

"I don't know, Priya. Somewhere between tea and samosas and rosogollas it was all decided and I really didn't have to say much. And then afterwards, it just seemed settled."

"What do you mean, 'It just seemed settled?'"

I knelt in front of him.

"They asked you, didn't they? Wasn't there a question in all of this?"

"Yes and no. Yes, they asked afterwards. But it wasn't really asking. You were there."

"I was there for the tea, Prem. I wasn't there for your answer."

"Well, they asked me afterwards and I said 'yes.'"

I imagined the tea party as I had witnessed it. In my

85

mind, I revived the stiff sarees and overdone makeup of the women, the men dressed in formal attire, the crisp white shirts and ironed colored ties. I remembered fingertips grasping fragile teacups, the tea steaming and scalding within. Prem had been seated between his parents, his mother's ample bosom and his father's ample stomach seeming to box him into the middle.

On the other side, across, she was seated between her father and sister. Her father was a slight man with exaggerated features and her sister was pristine and proper. For her part, she was sitting up straight, her kohl lined eyes cast downwards in a permanent gaze to the floor.

"What is your name, beta?" asked Prem's mother, although we all knew her name.

"Aasthika," she said almost inaudibly.

"What a beautiful name," Prem's father countered.

Silence.

"So Prem helps with the family business?" her father said after clearing his throat.

"Yes, yes," Prem's father stated.

Silence.

"Please have some samosa," Prem's mother gestured.

There were nods from Aasthika's father and sister but, other than that, all was still.

"Aasthika is a very good cook and artist. She paints very well," her father offered.

"Really? Well Prem here likes art very much," Prem's father said. "Don't you, Prem?"

Prem nodded.

Here I saw Aasthika look up surreptitiously, steal a glance at Prem, and then back down at the cool stone floor.

I lingered longer in the kitchen, watching, observing, wondering. I didn't realize I would endure an hour of the same pattern, the same ineffective conversations and awkward silences. And then, as if on cue, her father and sister rose simultaneously with, "Thank you so much for having us here. We are honored to have come."

"No, no," Prem's father insisted. "The pleasure was ours. What a beautiful and talented girl."

"Yes, and what a fine young man," her father stated. "Congratulations!"

"To you as well!" Prem's father's voice boomed.

Everyone rose except Prem, who, until nudged by his mother, sat and stared emptily at the wall.

"After they left," Prem said jarring my thoughts. "When you were clearing the plates and food and all of that. I went to the terrace. They both came up."

"And then what?"

"Then they said there were three possible dates for the wedding according to the priest and which would I prefer?"

I stopped pacing the room.

"That's what was said?"

"See, Priya it was all so fast and all so... so *settled*. So, when they said, 'Three months?' I said 'Yes.'"

I walked behind him and softly placed my hands on his shoulders.

"We'll think of something," I said.

Later, when I was alone, I researched the meaning of Aasthika as I had never heard the name before. I stared at the word as I read: *Faith*.

Chapter Nineteen

That Friday I walked into work early to enjoy breakfast in peace. I carried my McDonald's biscuit with bacon egg and cheese in a greasy bag with a hash brown and a small orange juice in my hand. But the store front was gleaming, and the gate was already up. I suspected that maybe Ed had gotten there to order jobs but then realized that although it was vaguely possible, it was probably not true. I walked in to find Sam in the doctor's office, rubber gloves on, Swiffer wet jet resting in a corner.

"Sam, what are you doing?"

"Isn't it obvious? I'm cleaning, Priya."

"Why? Is the cleaning lady dead?"

"Very funny," he smirked.

"Did you clean the windows out front too?"

"The windows. The door. The floor. Priya, I want this doctor to walk into 20/20 heaven."

"Sam, you can't be serious."

I rolled my eyes and set my breakfast and orange juice on the doctor's desk.

"Not there, Priya! That's a greasy bag. I can see it from here."

He waved his hands in the direction of the door.

"Go to my office. Make some coffee. Eat in there.

No one comes in here until Dr. Ibrahim comes in here."

"Oh, God, Sam, you're obsessed."

With that I went to his office and wondered if this doctor would be worth the fuss. I had never seen Sam so excited about a doctor but then we'd never had a new doctor. Dr. Bello had come with the practice and although Sam had "hired" her, he hadn't recruited her or found her in any way. She had said simply that she would stay for a price and Sam had weighed the benefits of having a familiar face and a credentialed optometrist versus spending time trying to find someone new who had to wait to be credentialed and who would take time garnering patient trust and thought it best to keep her. There was no fanfare in the decision and he certainly hadn't donned rubber gloves for anyone I knew. His excitement was contagious though and as I ate my breakfast, I found myself becoming quite excited at the prospect of a new doctor. After I finished, I leaned back in Sam's chair and pretended I owned the place. I wondered what it felt like to own 20/20 and even though Sam always referred to it as "ours," I had no stake in what was the biggest investment of my time and energy. I closed my eyes and leaned back.

"You can't sit in that chair until you earn it, kiddo."

I shot up at the sound of Ed's voice, my eyes peeled open.

"I was just—"

He started chuckling.

"Wanna be the big boss, do ya?"

"No, I just."

"Relax, Priya. Why're you so tense all the time anyway? Besides, you're the boss of me, kiddo!"

"Privilege," I said as I threw a packet of moist towelette in his direction and missed.

"You're here early," I said. "What a shocker."

"Ha. Ha. Ha. Come on, we have work to do. Sam wants this place ready and spotless for the new doctor."

"And you?"

Ed shrugged.

"I just hope she's pretty."

"That's the spirit," I said as I got off the chair and followed Ed to the front. We went through the pile of miscellaneous trays stacked in the right-hand corner of the counter. Most of them were things neither Ed nor I wanted to deal with, me because I honestly didn't know what to do with them and him because he was too lazy to do what needed to be done with them. One by one we dismantled the trays and made notes, phone calls, lab orders.

By 10:00 when we opened, the store was immaculate, and the counter was so decluttered it seemed that something was missing.

The day went fast and was so busy that even Ed had to sell. We both dealt with pleasant patients and problem patients alike and at the end of it all were tired yet felt successful. Just as we were about to close the door, a panicked kid came in wearing an NYU sweatshirt. He couldn't have been more than 20 and he looked absolutely horrified.

"Can we help you?" I asked.

"We're closed," Ed drawled.

"Please, Ed." I said. "Look at him."

"My glasses broke," said the kid. "I have a huge exam tomorrow. Please, please help me."

I stared past his shaggy black hair and saw in his eyes the same lost look that I had seen once before in a countenance. It made everything inside me constrict and although I wanted desperately to look away or, like Ed, to turn the kid away, I couldn't. I took the pieces of frame from his slender, trembling fingers and although I wanted to focus on the frames, on the lenses (which were miraculously intact without even a scratch), my mind travelled back 17 years to the look held by a shy boy who seemed like he was comfortable nowhere in the world.

"Let's try to find you a frame. Do you care which color?"

"Flaming red for all I care. I need to pass this exam."

I turned from him and held one of the lenses to various zyl frames trying to find a match. All the while, I remembered him looking longingly at Leyla, always longingly, yet lost in his ability to speak his mind or offer a word of confidence.

When I finally found a match, I turned hastily and showed him the frame.

"What do you know? It's black. It's practically identical to yours."

"Great! How much is it?"

"Two fifty."

His expression clouded, and, after some effort, he pulled a worn brown wallet from his jeans pocket. He counted bills, stared dejectedly at a credit card tucked into a sleeve.

"What is it?"

He looked at me, the loss in his eyes looking greater, his pupils looking rounder. I couldn't bear to look at him, so I looked away, waiting.

"I can only do $150," he said. "I can't pay that much. It's okay. Thanks anyway."

"Take it," I said without looking at him. I switched on the frame warmer and started inserting lenses into the frame.

"Take it? For $150?"

"Yeah, just take it," I said.

"Why?"

"What difference does it make?" I snapped as I snapped the right lens into place.

He said nothing as I knew he wouldn't but offered me three crisp $50 bills.

"I was saving this to take my girlfriend to dinner for her birthday," he said for no reason at all. "Guess she'll have to wait."

I looked at him quickly and saw the boyish grin, the flicker of desire in his eyes as he spoke of her.

I snapped the left lens into place and shut off the frame warmer. I cleaned the glasses, haphazardly threw the cleaning wipe on the counter and handed him the glasses. He put them on. He looked handsome and I knew that whoever loved him, this "her" that he spoke of, would love him the same way Leyla had loved Jay.

"Take it for $50," I said. "You can still take her out with $100."

With that I took one $50 bill from his royal flush of bills with my index finger and thumb, not disturbing the other two bills at all.

"Why?" he asked.

"Dude, just take the money and glasses and go."

"Thank you. Oh, my God, thank you. I'm going to tell everyone about you guys. Oh, my God you saved my life!"

"Just go."

"Thank you!"

When he tried to take my hand to shake it, I pulled away. He seemed confused, seemed to understand finally that I wanted him just to please leave and took a step back. He turned and left abruptly.

As the bells jangled and halted, Ed said "What the hell was that, Priya?"

"What do you mean?"

"What do I mean? Really? You're allergic to discounts, Priya. Fifty bucks? You wouldn't have given the average Joe 50 bucks *off*."

"It was a close-out frame, Ed. He paid more than cost anyway."

"Come on, Priya. Close out or not, you're a shark. I have never seen you discount more than 20 percent on anything. And then you looked like you saw a ghost or something. You okay there, kiddo? You're freaking me out."

I turned to Ed and wanted to say so much and yet could offer no explanation at all.

"We all have our ghosts, Ed. We all have our stories, us opticians, right?"

"Right…"

"Someday, I will tell you mine."

With that I went and locked the door, gazing out into the darkness, wondering where he had gone, hoping he could put a smile on her face with $100 dinner.

Chapter Twenty

*My initial thought had been to invite him to dinner.
But he declined mostly because he knew his mother,
my aunt, would chide him for wasting money even if it
was my money. So, we took our rice and fish curry and
fried potatoes steaming in steel plates, water in steel
glasses and a jar of pickled mangoes to the terrace
where we ate under the glow of a solitary 45 watt
bulb, the light casting green onto our faces.*

"You think you're never going to tell them?" I
asked.

My initial thought had been to invite him to dinner.
But he declined mostly because he shied away from life
and this was sure to be a confrontation. He and I had
never spoken much let alone "hello" and "hey." Mostly,
we both hovered around Leyla if we ever crossed paths.

"It's a difficult path," he said as he used his
fingers to debone and mash the flesh of the fish.

"So, you're just going to do what?" I asked.

He chewed, and I watched, waiting.

"Eat your food." He said. "It will get cold."

It was cold even though it was a late yet bright
spring afternoon when I walked to his dorm and rang
the buzzer, the same buzzer she had deliberated over
almost a year ago. I thought he would not let me in

after I rang the buzzer and announced myself. But impolite he was not even if removed from the life he lived. He buzzed me in and I shakily climbed the stairs to his room, my hands in fists at my sides.

His clean hand rested at his side as he used his right hand to scoop rice and curry into his mouth.

"You have to tell them," I insisted.

"Tell them what, Priya? That there's a man, a man? Do you know what his father did?"

"What's that?"

He swallowed, took the steel glass and took a gulp of water, curry and rice sticking to the steel as he set it down.

"He told his father about me. And his father threw him down the stairs. That's what happens, Priya. There is no 'telling,' no 'listening.' Maybe living in America, you forget these things. Here, it is a crime. We are a crime. And when you commit a crime and confess, there isn't talking, there is punishment."

I wanted to punish him for the misery in Leyla's soul. I wanted to act, to *do* something even though I wasn't even sure what I would say to him. I knocked on the door, waiting. I had the urge to turn, a sense of foreboding, a sense of the fact that this might not be my place. But for Leyla, any place was my place.

"We could be in a different place." I said. "If people just talked about it."

He waved his curried finger at me as if to chastise a child.

"No, Priya, we don't talk here. When we tell someone to leave engineering for burnt coffee, we don't talk. And you think we'll talk of this?"

"So what the hell are you going to do?" I asked as I mixed the curry and potato and fish in my plate. I

scooped it all into my mouth, the robust flavors hitting me all at once.

"I don't know!"

It wasn't a scream exactly but it was loudly said.

"Hey. How are you, Priya?" he said softly as he opened the door.

"Hey."

"Come in."

I walked in leaving the door slightly ajar.

He reached for the jar of pickled mangoes that had a perpetual spoon inside and placed some pulp and rind in his plate.

"Priya, just let it go. Please just let it go. I will marry a nice girl and have nice children. Not now maybe. But someday. But let this go. This is not your place."

I felt tears in my eyes for reasons I could not explain and as I tried to swallow some rice and fish, it seemed to be stuck in my throat like a ball.

I noticed his basketball sitting quietly in a corner of the room.

"What can I do for you, Priya?" he asked formally.

"What the hell's your problem, Jay?" I spat.

His eyes looked downwards.

"She has tried calling you, seeing you, and you run away. And you say you love her."

"And you say you love him," I said when the fish and rice finally traveled down my throat.

"What's love got to do with anything, Priya?" he asked, confused as he chewed.

I looked at him and realized his eyes were looking at me, but they were veiled with his insistence that this conversation could not happen. He didn't let me see hurt or pain or any of what I felt he must be feeling.

Born a day apart, I sometimes felt what he felt. I sometimes knew his heart although he thought I didn't. So, I knew he wouldn't let me in and would close this chapter in his life, as he had so many others, for the sake of other people, for the sake of people who said they loved him but failed always to understand him.

"I do love her," he said as his eyes met mine.

"Then why won't you see her? Why won't you talk to her?"

"Priya, I can't."

"Are you serious, Jay? *You can't*? That's your answer?"

He put his head upon his palms and rocked back and forth. I watched, unsure of what to do or say.

"Priya it all became so complicated."

"And so, you abandon her? Just leave her like that?"

I didn't know what I was hearing until he looked up and I saw that he was crying, his face looking like a child's face, his tears wild and streaming from his reddened eyes to his chin

"I was scared, Priya. I *am* scared. To be with her. To touch her again. To know it can all happen again."

Finally, "I'm scared, Priya."

He had stopped eating and had his head tilted back. He was looking at the sky and stars for answers to his twisted fate.

"I know," I said mostly for lack of anything else to say.

But I didn't know. I didn't know then the dualities he straddled, the sacrifices he made and not what they were but how they made him feel. I couldn't fathom the claustrophobia of his life.

"It feels claustrophobic, Priya, like the world's closing in on me. I love her. God, how can you… " he gulped for air, "how can you doubt that?"

"I don't doubt you," I say as I take his hand in a friendly gesture.

"I don't doubt you're scared." I say. "But there has to be a way for you not to marry a nice girl and have nice children."

He snorts a laugh. It is a slight relief that he can still laugh. Although it is the last laugh I ever heard from him. And I wondered after if anyone heard him laugh after that night of fish and rice and potatoes and revelations.

"That night," he said, "that night when she called you and didn't call me. If she had called me, Priya, I wouldn't have known what to do. I didn't want the baby. I didn't. But I didn't not want it either. All I know is I've always wanted her. Does that make any sense?"

"No," I said.

"No." he said. "There is no way to not marry a nice girl and have nice children. But it's okay, Priya. I will be good to her. I promise."

"I want to be good to her because I love her. But I am scared. I can't do this."

"You're scared? And her? What about her?"

"She has you."

His grip on my hand tightened a bit. His eyes were wild with pain and his fear was palpable in the small room. He moved closer to me and I thought of how much he looked like a lost child and how afraid he was. And although I wanted to be angry with him, I couldn't. I began to understand why she was not angry and how she still loved him. Although when I looked at his hand in mine, all I could think was that this is the hand he used to hold hers, to graze her body, to tickle her into laughter. This is the hand she loved, the feel of his palm, the slenderness of his fingers. And I was lost in these thoughts as he was staring at me. When I looked up, I saw his lips, the lips that spoke her name, the lips she had touched with her own. I kissed him.

I didn't kiss *him*. I kissed him thinking *this* is the tongue she craved, and these are the lips she wanted sliding across her face. I kissed him thinking of her, thinking of her lips grazing my face, fantasizing about the rhythm and feel of her tongue. My eyes were closed and as my hands traversed his body, I thought this is the body she wants upon her, next to her, with her. I thought of her neck as I touched his, smooth and slender and tender. I felt the muscles of his shoulders and thought of her neckless, shoulder-less blouse, her skin gleaming in the sunlight.

He leaned into me and I fell back onto the bed and he was on top of me and I felt the heat of his body as he started to kiss my neck and I thought back to her warmth as I lay a hand across her abdomen, aching and mourning the loss of something that was never meant to be.

I slowly opened my eyes and saw his face, his eyes closed, his mouth slightly open and it was as if I were awakening from a dream or a nightmare. I couldn't tell which.

"Oh, my God," I said.

"Oh, my God," the Universe echoed.

Except it wasn't the Universe but his roommate who stood at the door I had left ajar and Voice One, his roommate's girlfriend who stood next to him holding his hand in hers.

He and I scrambled to sit up and as he sat there, face flushed, his hardness evident despite his basketball shorts, I rose and nearly ran to the door, brushing past his roommate and Voice One and into the hallway where I felt vomit in my mouth. I couldn't. Not there. I had to get outside. I ran. I ran down the stairs missing a few, slipping and jumping until I reached the outside, by the buzzer that now held two different scenarios and I vomited.

In so many ways, I felt purged and yet in so many ways I felt as if I could never rid myself of all that was inside me. I knew that I was saved from voices forever after when the rumors spread, when the story of Priya wants to be Leyla's boyfriend became that Priya had befriended Leyla because she wanted to get to Jay. Yet my own voice started to speak, a voice I had silenced and kept quiet despite small rectangular rainbow flags and clipboards and hushed whispers. And my voice spoke not to anyone else but to me, asking me for definitions of friendship and desire and betrayal.

I had no dictionary for these words. I looked up at the sky, now a dusky haze of purple and gray and black as if it were bruised. I cried. I cried because I knew I had lost her in saving myself. I knew that rewriting a true story into a lie had saved me from whispers and rejection but she would reject me. But she would have rejected both stories, would she have not?

I felt I had lost her until I reminded myself I had never had her. Not in the ways I had desired. And finally, although I had no dictionary for any of the words that came to me, I admitted and wrote a definition for desire onto the parchment of my soul: Leyla.

Chapter Twenty-One

Monday, I arrived at work an hour before opening. I didn't have to by any means, Sam had only asked Ed and me to arrive at 9:30, a half hour before opening and the entrance of the grand Dr. L.M. Ibrahim. But I couldn't bear to type that morning. I hadn't touched my keyboard or glanced at my computer screen after the last time I had written, and I worried that I would never be able to. The screen showed a blank page with a cursor in the left-hand corner and I couldn't bear to turn it off nor could I bear to type anymore. So, after rising and coffee and a couple of cigarettes and showering and even washing my hair, I left for work instead of sitting in a swivel chair typing.

20/20 seemed expectant that morning, as if awaiting the arrival of something great, someone great. I believed Sam's energy had infused itself into his beloved 20/20 which it so often did. When he was eager about money, about stretching even the stretch goal, we did just that. And then, on days he was somber and mellow and wondered as to the fate of "the business," we would make little or no money or spend the day with nonsense customer issues which would further prove his mood to him and to us.

The way Sam loved 20/20 was incredible. "The

business" was his lifeblood, a living, breathing investment by all means. I thought back often to Ed telling me that opticians had stories and although I knew Sam's simple story of love and loss, I wondered what stories I did not know. I wondered why "the business" became his lover when he was so confident and capable and sometimes handsome. Was he jaded by people and excited by brick and mortar? Or was it just a natural inclination for him to love 20/20 as it was for Ed to "get a snack?"

I was lost in these nonsensical thoughts (anything other than think about the novel, about the last line and the name written on paper now) when the door clanged open and Ed entered.

"Why are you sitting in the dark, kiddo?" he said as he flicked on a light.

He was drinking a purple protein shake through a grand straw and he took a seat next to me.

"Something troubling you, kiddo?"

"No. Just waiting for this great doctor."

"L.M. Ibrahim. Sounds like an attorney," he said.

We laughed softly for no reason except that we were both nervous and anticipating someone new at 20/20 for the first time ever. Even though Dr. Bello had been unbearable at times, she had fit into our worlds and our lives and we were used to the monotony of her complaints and Sam's as well. Truth was, we didn't know how to incorporate a new life, a whole person into our midst. I realized that if Sam thought 20/20 was his love, so did Ed and I.

"I hope she's pretty," Ed teased.

"She'll be lovely," I said.

"Seriously, Priya, I hope she fits in, you know?

Bello may have been a beast with money, but she kept to herself, no harm done."

"I know."

He sucked at his straw making a gurgling sound as a foam of shake stayed settled at the bottom. We both glanced at the clock which said quarter to ten. Why was Sam not here?

"Why isn't Sam here?" I asked.

"I dunno, kiddo."

There was silence once again and I thought of the blank page on my computer screen. It made me uneasy. No sooner was I envisioning the screen that the door jangled and in walked Sam in the same Armani suit and pink shirt and tie he had worn when I first met him. His hair was gelled, and he smelled amazing.

"Wow, Sam!" I said.

He took a short bow.

"Thank you, thank you. Now that I have your attention, I want to tell you ladies and gentlemen, or lady and gentleman, that Dr. Ibrahim will be joining us at 20/20 this morning. I want us to be professional but warm. I want her to feel included. She's asking for a very fair price and she seems amenable to all the, you know, doctorly duties that she has. I believe she will be a willing change from bellowing Bello."

Ed and I chuckled with nervousness. I looked at the clock and it was nearing 10:00. I caught Sam looking at the clock as well and then frowning as if let down that Dr. Ibrahim would dare be late on her first day. I knew he saw everything anyone ever did at 20/20 as a personal affront and I felt a little sorry for him. Here he was talking her up and there she was, not even considerate enough to…

The door jangled as she pushed in. She entered, gently shut the door behind her. The bells wavered softly, a whisper of sound. And there she stood awkwardly, nervously, watching us stare at her.

Leyla.

Like a whirlwind of tenses, past became present and present seeped into past. All seams seemed to break and yet sew together to form a new reality, a new world where yes, it was true that a man was dead but new life was given to a friendship that had also seemed to die. And perhaps as he would be reborn although leaving grief in his demise, so a friendship would rise like a phoenix from the ashes, resurrected as the present and shedding a past of confusion. All I had thought for the past few weeks crashed together and there was the rope and death and then her and me in a twin bed being friends and endings and beginnings, but I had to still my thoughts or else I would go crazy.

There she was, and she was magnificent, self-assured, as beautiful if not more than the day she sat swiveling in my silly apartment not knowing what to say. My heart did its one-sided dance of constriction and release, excited and frightened to be in her presence, in the presence and pretense of all I thought I had left behind only to give life to in half-written novels. But this story was now full of life and now we were both in the same room sharing air and light and sound. I had no words, but my eyes could not leave her as my soul had never left her and I rubbed my thumb slightly over her name that had rested unpeacefully on my wrist in red ink for years and years. My wrist seemed to glow with heat and I felt my face flush to a slight red. I tugged at my shirt sleeve unknowingly. And yet, still, I stared at her.

She looked from Sam to Ed. To me. To me. And her eyes stopped roaming the room.

"Priya?" she asked although she knew.

Her eyes stopped upon me as if she were in a trance. Perhaps she too traveled to the past and back realizing that love leads back to love even if the dance on both sides is not the same, one being a fast-paced trot and another a waltz. But we had danced together for all our awkwardness, had grown together and had laughed and cried together. We had shared love however incongruous in shape and form, me desiring and drinking her essence and she loving, me as her best friend, as a confidante without whom life lacked sap and substance.

"Priya," I repeated as if my own name were foreign to me.

"You know each other?" Sam said as he pointed at her and then at me.

"We used to study together. In college." I offered.

It was not a lie, but it felt like a lie upon my tongue.

Sam clasped his hands together in delight.

"Small world," he said, shaking his head from side to side.

"I'm Ed," said Ed as he extended a bulky hand.

She took his hand and moved it up and down slowly for a bit. Then she let go and stood quietly watching our performance, taking in what she could. I wondered if she were thinking back to college, to us, to our story, or if she were forcing herself to stay in the present, at 20/20, looking at an assortment of fools. But then I had allowed she and I to become us. She had never constructed an us. So perhaps she couldn't think back to something that, in reality and essence, never was and that existed only in the crevices of my being and belief.

"Dr. Ibrahim. Leyla. I'm—I'm pleased to meet all of you," she finally offered.

The same voice. The same voice that guided me through constellations on a hill in Vermont on starry nights. The same voice that spilled grief in words over the loss of a child that was never meant to be. The same voice I recited within myself every time I read the note she had slipped under the door to my apartment. Not a lengthy letter, not a demand for an explanation, just a simple note that read:

Priya—Home is where you go when your heart is broken. Returning to family in Atlanta. Love you, Leyla

I had read the note many times, pausing to imagine each word in her voice. Every time I read and heard the words, I could imagine her saying all but the words "Love you, Priya." Those words I always confused with "Love him, Priya."

"Priya, where'd you go?" Sam said jarring me from my thoughts.

"Yeah?"

"I said, 'Show Dr. Ibrahim her office.' Priya is my right hand, the manager of the whole place really," Sam said as he waved his hand like a benediction in the air.

"Let me show you," I said as I walked towards the office.

I heard her heels click delicately on the hardwood. When I reached the office, I flicked on the light and entered. She entered as well and stopped and looked around.

"It's great," she said.

"Hope you like it. And if you need anything—"

"I'll ask you," she said with a smile.

That smile. I had not seen a smile like that smile for 17 years. I drank in her presence more than I felt it. Her perfume wafted to me and it was no Exclamation. It was a woodsy, musky scent that suited her musky, mysterious self. She had grown so gracefully into adulthood and I? I felt inadequate to say the least. I looked down at my black sweater and pants that juxtaposed her crisp red linen shirt and pressed white pant suit. I felt somewhat out of place.

"Priya?"

"Yes?"

I looked at her and she looked back. I didn't know what to say with my voice or what to do with my hands. I placed them behind my back and clasped them together.

"This will be great." She finally said. "Sam seems like a great guy and Ed seems really nice."

"And me?" I said before I could stop the words.

"And you." she said as she smiled her crescent smile. "And you."

She walked to me and grazed my cheek slightly with the back of her hand.

"You were my best friend." she said. "How I loved you. You were my greatest strength, Priya. Through everything."

"I was what?"

"My best friend. We're going to rock this place," she said.

I heard the door jangle closed and left her office mumbling something about having to get to work.

All I remembered as I worked that day was her note. And how, after reading it, every plane I ever saw in the sky seemed to me to carry her home to heal her heart. And all planes flew to Atlanta.

Chapter Twenty-Two

It was a week after I met him when she and I finally met, when we finally spoke. I was reciting Chaucer, pacing the floor, memorizing lines I barely understood when my apartment bell buzzed. I opened the door to her, allowing her once again into my heart and life. Although I knew full well that she had never left.

"Do you know how hot it is outside?" she said.

"No," I answered as I shut the door behind her.

"It's cool in here," she offered.

With the door shut, we stopped speaking of the weather. In fact, we stopped speaking at all. She made her way to my study chair, a rickety plastic with a fabric back that swiveled from side to side and was surprisingly comfortable. She sat, planted her feet on the floor and swiveled gently from right to left. I stood and watched, at a loss of words and actions.

"How are you?" she asked as if we had not spoken for months.

"I'm well."

"'Well.'" Then "That's the English major in you. Most of us would just say 'good'."

"I guess."

Swivel right. Swivel left. Swivel right. She was driving me crazy.

I didn't know what to say to her but I knew I couldn't meet her eyes.

"I'm thinking of going away," she finally said and my chest constricted to a point where I thought it would never expand again.

"Why?"

I regretted the question as soon as it was released.

She looked at the floor, then at her sandals, her toes perfectly polished in a French pedicure and visible at the top. She had beautiful feet, I thought.

"Why not? I think I might just finish my degree elsewhere."

"You have so little time to go."

"Too much to be here," she said.

I wanted to tell her how I never touched him, how I tried to touch her through him but it would be a worse admission than what she thought. If she thought anything at all because as it were, she didn't speak of it although I was sure she knew.

"The heart wants what the heart wants," I said.

I didn't even know what I meant by it or why I said it. It was just a beautiful detour of words and it seemed apt.

I met her eyes for the first time that afternoon as she looked at me and smiled. It was a crescent smile, genuine and warm but I didn't know her thoughts and I wish I did.

"The heart," she said, "breaks sometimes. You have to put it back together."

Had I broken her heart? Or had he? Or had it broken of its own accord? I wanted answers to questions I was much too afraid to ask.

"Would you like some lunch?"

"No." she said. "I have to go. But I thought I'd stop by."

With that she rose quickly and abruptly walked to the door. Before I could offer a word, she was out, the door shut behind her. And I stood, my chest a big ball of confusion and regret, not realizing that her scent and her voice and her face were privileges I would not know for 17 years to come and she would meld my pasts and presents together forever. For such was her magic and the kind and unkind fate of the Universe. Leyla.

Chapter Twenty-Three

Leyla fit beautifully into the mechanics of 20/20. Ed couldn't stop raving that she was indeed "pretty" and he seemed to enjoy just being around her. Sam seemed lighter, more relaxed. And me? I avoided her as much as was possible. I justified it to myself by stating that I hadn't interacted much with Dr. Bello either. But I also knew that I hadn't gone out of my way to avoid her. And while Dr. Bello had stayed in her office with the door shut the majority of the time she didn't have a patient, Leyla stayed out front with Ed and me, watching us work, offering an anecdote sometimes about her travels or a patient she had seen.

It's funny how the heart learns to unclench. When I had known her, whenever I had seen her or been in her presence, my chest had felt as if it were tightening, as if there would soon not be air to breathe. When I saw her now, true I couldn't look directly at her, but that initial innocence of the heart was not there. I wondered about her, I had lists of questions I wanted to ask her, but my heart beat rhythmically, unfazed.

When Sam came for his regular Tuesday visit, he was wearing a charcoal suit with a lilac shirt and tie. Again, the hair gelled. Again, the wafting of some fantastic cologne. It seemed the hiring of Dr. Ibrahim had infused some life into him and breathed life into 20/20 itself. As it was, we were busier and patients were actually stating that "the exam was great!" which was something that was foreign to us in the times of Dr. Bello.

"Priya, got a minute?" Sam said knowing that he was actually instructing, not asking me to go to his office.

"Sure," I said.

Ed smiled and waved at us as we headed back. When we settled into our customary seats, Sam in his plush leather chair and me in the skimpy chair across, Sam folded his hands on the table.

"So is she as great as I imagine?" he said.

"She's good," I said.

"Good? Priya, look at the *numbers*. The numbers don't lie. We had better sales last week than in the past four months."

"Coincidence?"

"Priya!"

He sat back and placed his hands behind his head.

"You said you guys went to college together. Were you friends?"

"We knew each other," I said as I felt my face flush, as my heart betrayed me and stopped beating rhythmically and started its dance of clenching again.

"Listen." he said as he shot forward. "I want you to take her to lunch. My treat. Take her somewhere nice."

"What?"

"Take her to lunch. Make her feel welcome."

"Sam, there is so much work to do with ordering and inspecting and what if patients walk in?"

"I'll man the floor with Ed."

"You?"

"Yes, Priya, me. I can sell snow to a polar bear. You aren't the only one with the gift of sales, you know."

I played with my thumbs.

"Priya, look, I would do it but it's awkward. It might seem like I'm hitting on a married woman and that's the last thing I want her to think."

I looked up at him.

"Married?"

"Yes, she's married. Told me that at the interview. Not that I asked. But she said she had moved back to Atlanta before SUNY then moved back to New York from Atlanta after some time, something about her husband."

I should have realized she was married because she hadn't been "Ibrahim" in college. She had been Madhuvati. Leyla Madhuvati. Somehow the reality of her last name had slipped my mind.

"So, will you do it?"

Before I could agree or disagree, Sam pulled out his wallet and slid his Platinum American Express across to me.

"Anything she wants. Anything you want. Just, no liquor."

"Yeah Sam, I was about to get wasted on company time."

He shrugged.

"Just saying. I don't want to be responsible when you say, 'but you never said.'"

"Where should I take her?"

"Ask her. Anywhere she wants. Just be back in an hour. An hour and a half. Be back in an hour and a half."

I slowly took his card and rose. I placed the card in my pocket.

"Priya?"

"Yeah, Sam?"

"Thank you. Thank you so much."

"Sure."

When I knocked on her office door, she opened it instantly as if she had been waiting for me all the while.

"So sorry, I was talking to my husband. He's under the weather today. Do we have a patient? Have they been waiting long?"

"No, no. I—Sam—"

A slight clench, like an open palm aching to become a fist.

"Sam?"

"Sam suggested we go to lunch, you and I. I was wondering if you'd like to and what you would like."

"I'd love to, Priya."

"What would you like?" I asked as I fiddled with Sam's credit card.

"Sushi? Is there decent sushi here?"

"Sure. I mean Indian is king around here but there is decent sushi."

"Great. Let me get my bag and we can go. I mean are we going now?"

"Yes, now. If you are hungry now."

She looked in the mirror and ran her fingers through her hair. I remembered quickly (and then the thought returned to wherever it had come from) her hair fanned across a pillow as she lay next to me on a blanket, waiting for the stars to shine upon us.

"Let's go," she said.

She stopped at the counter and waved at Ed.

"Priya's taking me to lunch," she said.

"Priya never took me to lunch," Ed said as he feigned a pout.

"Come on, Ed, we've had lunch together."

"Never *outside*," he said.

"Because we can't both leave at once," I said.

He shrugged and then smiled and waved.

"Have a great lunch. Are you having Indian?"

"No." I said. "But I can bring back some chicken biryani. Sam's treat."

"That's why you're the best, kiddo!"

I watched Leyla watch us and she was smiling at our exchange.

We walked out, the door jangling behind us, and stood just outside 20/20.

"Which way?" she asked.

I didn't answer but started walking to the right and she followed.

Chapter Twenty-Four

"How did you become an optometrist?" I asked as I took a sip of water.

"Seemed like the right thing at the right time," she said.

"You wanted to be a cardiologist. To heal hearts, remember?"

She tilted her head slightly as she laughed.

"You remember, Priya. Yes, I did. But once I moved back to Atlanta, things changed. I changed. My family life changed. And this became a viable and sensible option."

"A viable and sensible option," I repeated.

I pretended to look at the menu although I knew I would order an Alaskan roll and California roll. But the pretense of the menu kept me from looking at her and I had to keep from looking at her, so I didn't ask the questions I wanted answers to. Questions far removed from optometry.

"I think I'll have the three-roll special." she said. "And some miso soup."

I nodded.

"What about you?"

"Um, I think the Alaskan and the California. And some miso soup."

After we ordered, the waiter removed our menus. My hands felt empty. I tore the packet of chopsticks and started twirling the paper.

"Do you ever wish you hadn't moved back to Atlanta? In college, I mean?"

She was silent for some time, her eyes looking at me but worlds away.

"I had to," she said.

"Because of me?"

She looked out of the window and I watched her, wondering what her eyes settled on, whether it was the red delivery moped just outside or a passerby. When she looked back at me, it was I who looked away. She placed her hand on mine, a warm delicate hand with a bright blue sapphire on her ring finger with a small diamond on either side, all square, all elegant and beautiful. Like her. Like her.

"Priya."

I looked at her and she trapped my gaze with hers and I had nowhere else to look except into her bright hazel eyes.

"We were young, Priya. We were foolish. I never left because of you. I left because I had to for me. Just to have new air, new space."

I felt my eyes begin to prick with tears. My throat felt raspy.

"Priya, whatever happened, we were kids. We were young. I never ever held any of it against you."

"You know then?"

"That you went to see him on my behalf and ended up making out?"

It sounded so trifling and silly the way she said it that I laughed despite myself, the tears receding, relief rising.

"Well, when you say it like that, I mean—"

118

"Priya, I didn't leave because you made out with my boyfriend. Is that what you thought?"

I had never thought of it as "making out with her boyfriend" but as a transgression, as betrayal and I had envisioned her hurt, her anger, her pain. Because what she didn't know is that I never "made out with her boyfriend" but made out with her through her boyfriend and if she knew that, perhaps she would not be as gracious.

"Then why did you leave? I mean you say for you but why?"

"Because my heart was broken, Priya. Not just by a person. Just by life in general. My spirit was broken. I couldn't stand being in the same places. And because I knew I was breaking hearts too. I don't expect you to understand."

"Well, that's quite patronizing."

She squeezed my hand. My beating heart skipped a beat and that beat escaped like sound, invisible into the air, a duo of quarter notes in a deep bass, Ley-la.

"I'm sorry, I didn't mean for it to be patronizing."

Our soup came. I played with the spoon and swirled the soup around, the seaweed entangling itself on the spoon.

"Priya, back then, oh how I loved him. His silence killed me. But he didn't break me. I just... I just broke."

I blew softly on a spoonful of miso before I put it in my mouth.

"I thought I broke you," I finally said.

"You? You were my best friend, Priya. My strength. I thought you knew that. You were the reason I contemplated staying. But at the end of it, it all became kind of messy, didn't it?"

I didn't know what she meant by "messy." All I knew was that if her spirit had been broken, so had mine. So, I did understand what she was saying but I couldn't tell her because, ironically, if what had kept her fractured spirit held together was that she had loved me, what had broken my spirit was that I loved her. And that was something I could never say or let her know.

"I was afraid I would break you," she said.

"I'm sorry?"

She folded her hands in front of her and looked radiant. Her eyes met mine and across the single candle glowing orange on the table, her eyes were mellow and kind.

"How you loved me," she said. "And how I took advantage of that love. I was afraid that if I didn't leave, I would break you. And Priya I loved you too much, you were too good for me ever to be the reason you broke."

I had no words for her. I had no defense, no argument. Because I did love her. And had she stayed, perhaps I would have broken, exploded, deteriorated. I knew that. Even then, when I missed her, I knew her essence would have killed me. But I survived albeit with her name tattooed across my wrist like fire.

"You knew?" I whispered because I was about to cry. It was as if her footsteps were treading lightly upon my clenched heart, heavily upon the parchment of my soul.

"I knew. Even you didn't know for most of it. But I knew."

"And?"

"'For I love and this love was your gift.'"

I smiled despite myself.

"You remember?" I said.

"The night you read St. Augustine's *Confessions* all at once for the paper due in the morning? And I lay on your bed as you reached that line. Recited that line. Said it again. 'Page 236,' you said. I remember, Priya. I may not have loved you as you loved me but I loved you. Love does not have to be equal or cut of the same fabric, Priya. But it's there. It was there. You were my best friend. And for that I loved you. And was grateful. And selfish."

I looked away towards the window, a slight haze of mist descending from the sky, the clouds rolling gray.

"Sam tells me you're married," I said to the window.

"I am."

I looked at her and smiled a pale smile.

"L.M. Ibrahim," I said in my most professional voice. "Leyla Madhuvati Ibrahim. Dr. Leyla Madhuvati Ibrahim."

She smiled back at me as she took some soup with a spoon.

"What does he do?"

"Do?"

"Your husband."

"Raza? He's looking for work. I mean we just moved here a few months ago so he's looking."

Something in the fidget of her eyes told me she wasn't telling me everything. But what she wasn't telling me I couldn't know.

"What kind of work does he do?" I asked.

"Various things. This sushi is amazing."

I felt certain she didn't want to speak of him.

"It's good," I said.

We ate silently with chopsticks. I did not bring up Raza again.

121

Chapter Twenty-Five

Again, the thunder sounded although there was no rain to follow. I lay in my bed reciting, "Leyla Madhuvati Ibrahim" as if it were a prayer and not a name. My thoughts took me back to clearer skies.

Again, he looked in the mirror and adjusted his tie although it hadn't moved. The day of the wedding had arrived. Although I had promised Prem that we would do something, nothing had occurred except that a week had passed and I had returned to New York and then come back again 11 and a half weeks later for his wedding.

He looked downright handsome in his suit. It was an olive color, the material firm and unrelenting. His shirt was a soft cream linen shirt, the collar gentle against his blazer and he had a silk, cream tie to match. He had shaved yet had left a firm and thin mustache above his thick lips. It made him look like a mature man although his eyes, if I looked into them, were those of a scared young boy.

"You look handsome," I said.

When he looked at me, he looked so lost that I had to look away.

"I feel bad for her, Priya," he said.

I walked to him and held him. In my arms, he felt

frail although he was broad and strong and full of life. I didn't know what to offer him. I didn't know what dialogues we should share.

"You're the only brother I know," I said.

When I pulled away and he was at arm's length, I saw tears swimming in his eyes.

"I'll be good to her, I promise."

"I don't doubt it."

The wedding itself was one of pomp and glamour, with him being the only son and her being the younger daughter. There was much talk and much food and many photos and through it all, Prem endured.

I have a photograph on my fridge still of him and Aasthika, neither smiling but both looking at each other, her in a striking red sari with gold trim, him in his olive-green suit with cream underneath, asking in a gaze, perhaps, if they had made the correct decision for the rest of the fate of their lives.

Chapter Twenty-Six

"I'm telling you, I can't see. It's all wavy. Like water."

"And I'm telling you," I said as gently as those words could be said, "that you need to practice with the progressives."

"Practice? What kind of bullshit is that? This isn't a tournament. They're glasses."

I sat back in my chair. Although I had handled many difficult situations at 20/20, now I knew I had an audience. Leyla, unlike Dr. Bello, would watch me work and this made it increasingly uncomfortable. Although the clenching of the heart was not a normalcy as it had been in college, it came and went. And when she watched me work, I wanted to impress her, to show her my character as strong and yet compassionate.

"I promise you'll leave here happy." I finally said. "But please just work with me. You're going from glasses for just distance where there is one power in the entire lens to progressive where the lens *progressively* shifts power from distance to reading. Your eyes need to adjust. If you could just look across the room for me."

"It's fucking blurry."

"More your head down slowly, slightly. Keep your eyes just where they are. Better?"

A grunt. That meant it was better but the patient (an emerging 40 something year old male) would rather not say because, of course, it was better. Glasses were science. There was always a way to make them work. Somehow, people wearing them always tried to challenge that notion and made them subjective.

"Now look at me."

"You're blurry."

"Move your head up a little more. Just a bit. Better?"

A slight nod. So much better than a grunt.

"Now here's a reading card." I said as I handed him the story of good old Ben inventing bifocals.

"It's—"

"I know. It's blurry. Keep your eyes down and move your head up slowly, very slowly until it all comes into focus."

"Uh."

"Good?"

"So, wait?" Here he looked up at me and himself, consciously or unconsciously, adjusted his head until I came into focus.

I noticed the bristles of gray at his temples, small porcupine spikes of hair that he hadn't bothered taming or dyeing.

"Yes?"

"I gotta move my head all the time?"

"No, it becomes more natural with time. When you go home, try to watch TV and read a newspaper or magazine at the same time. That'll force your eyes to use multiple focal points and you'll get used to them faster. Be very careful with curbs and stairs for the first week or so or until you put them on and it just seems natural to you."

"What if I try them and hate them?"

I sighed sharply.

"There are no refunds as every product is custom made."

"So," he said as he leaned forward, "I'm shit out of luck?"

"Not if you like them."

He started to say something and then stopped. He got up, flung on his jacket and grabbed the maroon 20/20 case I had laid open on the counter. He jammed his glasses into it with some violence, snapped the case shut, put it in his jacket pocket.

He paused. Then, for reasons I didn't know why, he smiled.

"Thank you so much. You've been great. And I'm sorry if I was a bit rough around edges. First time with these damn things, you know?"

"No worries." I said. "Glad you're happy. Thanks for shopping at 20/20."

"Thank you," he said.

He flung the door open much wider than he had to and then exited. The bells jangled vehemently.

"Great job, Priya," Leyla said.

I liked her praise. She had noticed. But I also felt like she was patronizing me, telling me I did a good job as if this were not my job, as if I hadn't repeated this performance in all its variations a thousand and one times for different people.

"Thanks." I stated flatly.

"She's a tough one." Ed said as he walked to me and placed a hand on my shoulder. "She's our negotiator."

Leyla laughed a slight laugh.

"I loved how you turned him around. He started off so badly and by the end he was thanking you. That's amazing."

I nodded in her direction but didn't say anything. I tugged at my shirt sleeve trying to cover her name glowing in bright red across my wrist. I wish I could show her, say something like "I always carried you with me because I always loved you even when I didn't know I loved you." But such dialogues were not permissible, and I knew that. So, all I did instead was tug at my sleeve so that the red was covered, and her name stayed hidden under a shirt sleeve cuff just as it had within me for as long as I had known her.

For no reason that I could know, she walked to the back of my chair and placed her palms on my shoulders. I had thought that my heart had stopped its silly game of constricting but there it was again, a knot in my chest demanding attention.

"I'm proud of you," she said. "Proud of who you have become."

"You don't know me," I said hastily as I pulled at my shirt sleeve, held the edge of the sleeve in a fist and rose to put a patient's tray on the back counter to be ordered.

Truth was, she knew me better than I knew myself or my heart and this frightened me. Because 17 years had passed and we had gone from past college kids to present adults and my heart still held her close, desired her close and even if I lied and said that the muscle of my heart didn't clench for her, it did. Over and over and over. Every time I saw her or heard her or was touched by her. Such was her magic still 17 years after what I thought was the last time I had seen her. Leyla.

Chapter Twenty-Seven

October was my favorite month of the year although it was a deceptive month. While the sun shone brightly promising warmth, the days were so crisp it seemed they might break under the tension. The evenings came quickly and darkened the city all at one with no warning sometimes. Sometimes October brought flurries though rarely but often it brought a cold rain that seeped well into me and left me cold the entire day regardless of the jacket or hat I wore. This was one of those wet, gloomy days where the sun stubbornly refused to emerge, and the clouds rolled fast and gray overhead.

I had gotten to work before the rains began and I was checking jobs in the lensometer when the rumble of skies took me by surprise and a heavy rain descended onto the entire city slashing the door and windows. I stopped turning the power drum and looked outside marveling at a New York monsoon. I hadn't thought about him in days but then he descended as well into my mind, a boyish smile over some chai as we shared Parle-G biscuits and Springsteen bellowed in the background. I was thinking and trying to remember the song that was playing when I heard Leyla's heels on the hardwood.

"What is that sound?" she asked. "Oh my God, look at the rain!"

"It's coming down really hard," I said as I smiled slightly.

I had mastered the slight smile in the past few months that I had maneuvered around her. Ed came from the bathroom and stood next to Leyla staring at the sky through the windows.

"Oh my God, kiddo. It's like a monsoon. Is this what a monsoon is like?"

"Somewhat," I answered.

I tried to concentrate on the glasses in front of me. Minus two. Minus 250. Axis 180. Seemed about right. It was perfect actually. I marked the lenses and just as I raised the lens stop to mark the left lens, we were submerged in darkness.

"What the fuck?" I said without meaning to.

"Language, kiddo. Not fucking appropriate in front of the doctor especially," Ed said as he chuckled, as he always did, at his own joke.

"Seems like the power's out," Leyla said.

"Brilliant deduction," I said.

"Deduction," she said as she laughed slightly. "The words you use."

"I think it should come on soon." Ed said. "But if not, I think I have candles somewhere."

He went to find candles and I stared outside, the only light being the flashes of lightening that chose to interrupt the torrents of rain.

"Are you okay?" Leyla asked.

"Me? Yes, I'm fine."

We stood in silence staring at the rain each thinking different thoughts although we shared space.

"I found birthday candles," Ed said as he returned.

"Because they'll last long," I said.

"We have a bunch of them, kiddo. We'll light a few at a time. It's just us anyway. I doubt any moron would venture out to get glasses in this."

"Don't doubt the morons, Ed," I said.

This elicited a laugh from Leyla who took a seat at the dispensing counter as Ed took a tray and lit a candle. He dripped some wax into the tray and then planted the candle in the wax. He repeated this, as I watched, a total of six times until there was a ball of glow from the candles that illuminated Leyla's eyes.

"Can't we close?" I asked.

"Wait it out, kiddo. Wait it out. Besides, you don't want to venture out in this anyway. Where are you going to go with the rain coming down like that?"

I took a seat across from Leyla. Ed rolled a chair next to her and sat as well.

We were silent save our breathing which seemed loud in the darkness. The rumble and grumble of the skies continued. Leyla looked down at her phone and then back at us. I discerned a half frown in the glow.

"What's wrong?" I asked.

"Nothing. Just—just my husband. I hope he's okay."

"He's a grown man, doc." Ed said. "He can make do with a little rain. How long have you been married?"

"Ten years."

"And still the puppy love, worrying about him in the rain," Ed joked.

Leyla smiled but her eyes did not.

"Just—just worried," she nearly whispered.

"Call him," I suggested.

She looked to meet my eyes as if telling me something that I couldn't understand then looked away and said, "No. No. It's best I don't."

We were silent then, casting shadows across the hardwood and counters. Ed was leaning back with his arms folded. Leyla cradled her phone. And I sat with my hands folded in front of me, forgetting that my sleeves were not long. In the glow of the flames, I felt my tattoo glow brighter although in reality it loomed dark upon my wrist.

"What do we talk about?" Ed said.

"What do you want to talk about?" Leyla asked.

They turned to me and I looked from one to the other. Ed's glasses reflected the tiny candle flames as did Leyla's eyes. I locked my gaze at her eyes and wished I could travel into her mind through that gaze. But while there was warmth and pain in the look her eyes held, there lay no invitation there.

"What we talk about when we talk about love," I finally said.

"I love that story, kiddo," Ed said.

"You know it?" I asked surprised.

"I know more than you think I know, kiddo. Of course I know it. My wife—"

Here the air died. It simply died in darkness and there was no sound save the torrent outside. Leyla and I looked at each other, at him, then at each other again. Someone had to say something. But what was there to say?

"Tell me about her," Leyla said gently.

Ed sat still.

131

Then, "Well, doc, it was a humble story really."

"Every humble story bears a great and grand love," Leyla said as if she knew this by admissions of her own heart.

I wondered then about Ed but also about her and her great loves. Had there been many or few? Had she ever loved and lost? Had she known heartbreak beyond Jay?

"Tell me your story, Ed. You promised you would," I said.

"Kiddo, let's just leave it."

"Why?" Leyla asked.

"Because she's dead," Ed said forcefully.

His breathing became deeper, short breaths that seemed to leave plumes of despair in the darkness.

"Ed," Leyla said softly, "talking about her doesn't make her any more dead or alive."

"I miss her," he finally said.

"What do you miss?" Leyla asked.

Ed sat back and crossed his arms, shuffled his feet and cleared his throat. I wondered if finally he would tell me about her and was amazed that Leyla could elicit from him after three months what I couldn't in three and a half years. But then such was her magic, her charm. And I sat charmless and listening and waiting as Ed started to speak.

Chapter Twenty-Eight

"It was a different world back then." Ed began. "College was cheap. We didn't have cell phones or computers or distractions. We had people. We noticed people. And I noticed her many times when my buddies and I went to the diner to have burgers. I thought maybe they had sections, so I always sat at the same table. And she always came over. Always smiled.

'I was a freshman. I was only 18 and I knew she was older. She seemed older. I loved her accent; it was a Southern drawl that made her hold onto words just a little longer than she had to. And she smelled amazing. Kiddo, there isn't a perfume made today that can compare to the way she smelled.

'It was six months of burgers before I asked her to a movie. Six months. Back then, things went slow. And I was 18. I didn't know the first thing about a date or asking a girl out. I'd never had a high school girlfriend. I'd gone to prom with my best friend's sister. Mildred was the first girl I actually asked out. And she said 'Yes. Why I'd love to.'

'Today, these people date 10-20 people before they 'find' someone. Me, I knew. I knew Milly was my girl and would be my girl. I think she knew too.

'We became inseparable. When I wasn't studying, I was with her. Even while I was studying, I'd take my table by the window and she'd serve me coffee all night while I worked. We were in our own world. We made a space for us and we were happy."

Here Ed leaned back just a little, exhaled loudly. I looked to Leyla who was looking at him as if eliciting more, mesmerized by his simple story.

"So, what happened?" she finally asked.

"What happened, doc, is that I wanted to marry her. And her parents were dead set against it because she was five years older. Five. In those days, these things mattered. And my parents thought I should see more of the world before marrying the first girl I loved. But we did it anyway. The day I graduated, we went to town hall and got married. No big wedding for us. We didn't need anyone. And we moved into a small studio because that's what we could afford.

'For our honeymoon, we went to the Jersey shore."

Here he chuckled as if at a joke only he was privy to.

"The Jersey shore," he said again. 'Don't get me wrong, we had a great time. But of all the places we wanted to go, that's the only place we could afford to go. So off we went. We swam. And ate. And made love. Back then, it seemed like the first of so many vacations we would take. It ended up being the only one.

'I got a job on Wall Street, you see. Back then, even though there wasn't the craziness that's there today, Wall Street was still crazy. I worked long hours. She worked long hours. I wish now that we had spent more time together. But we were busy trying to make it. And we made it. We moved into a nicer place. Had nicer things. Had everything but the time to actually be together."

Here he paused again. This time, neither of us spoke and we simply waited for the rest. The candles flickered but stayed bright. They were halfway melted into the tray.

"Then, one year became two became three." He said. "And then, a week after our fourth anniversary, we were having breakfast on a Sunday and she fell to the floor. Just like that. Turns out, she had an aneurysm. It was random. I could have done nothing, they said. Imagine that. Thirty. And dead.

"I'm always glad I met her and loved her. But you know what? There was no one ever like her again. Maybe it's me. Maybe I'm old fashioned. These days, people get married two/ three times. But me? After Milly, there was no one who made love worthwhile."

It was a much simpler story than I had anticipated. But then, Ed was a simple man. It struck me how sometimes we forsake love and yet more often than not, great love is taken from us. And perhaps what makes love great is not its magnitude or drama but how it makes us feel.

Outside, the skies roared with peals of thunder and lightning slashed the dark afternoon. Inside 20/20, Leyla and I sat without words, waiting.

Ed said nothing more.

Chapter Twenty-Nine

When the candles were nearly burnt out, Ed arranged another half dozen in the tray and lit them. Once again, there was a soft glow. The rain had steadied but the thunder still rolled in the sky and flashes of lightening interrupted the darkened afternoon. I looked at Leyla and wanted to keep looking at Leyla. When she caught me, I simply moved my gaze to Ed.

"So, Doc, that was my story. What's yours?" Ed asked.

His eyes were far away but he forced them upon us, tucked away all the thoughts he had brought to the surface because, if he hadn't, I am sure his heart would have collapsed.

Leyla shifted in her chair.

"Who's this man that's kept your heart for ten years?"

Leyla sat back and smiled slightly but there was hesitation in her. I was becoming curious now as well to her story, to life after college and Jay. I started wondering without meaning to how her husband had proposed, how he had had the sense to know that he should.

"Doc?" Ed said.

"Nothing to tell," she said.

"Oh come on, I told you." Ed joked. "Tell us how you met. What he does. Why you love him so much that a little rain scares you to be without him."

Leyla sighed. She fondled her pendant, a silver piece that resembled a book. Her silence told me what her words never had; that there was something she was not telling us. My mind spiraled thinking of possibilities.

"Tell us," I said.

She looked at me and nodded slowly, gently.

"Okay." She said. "Okay."

Ed and I leaned in because her voice was soft, and we could barely hear her words.

"I met Raza in New York at an art gallery in Soho. He's an artist. He paints all these wonderful things. My friends and I were passing by and he had this one painting in the window. And I fell in love with the painting—"

I missed part of what she said because when her voice said "I fell in love" my heart constricted, and the words echoed inside me. I had never heard her say it, not for Jay or for anyone that had touched her life. I forced myself to pay attention again.

"Raza does work with paint and words. I think that's what I love about his work. That's what I told him when I met him. The first thing I said to him was 'I'm in love.' I meant to finish by saying 'with your work' but seeing him, I just couldn't talk any more than that."

"Wow, Doc, that's what I call love," Ed said.

Leyla smiled and this time her eyes shone.

"He asked me out for coffee and I went. He's a charming man when he wants to be. When he can be," she said, and the light left her eyes. Now, the look in her eyes resembled the storm outside, deep and dark and

137

mysterious. She shook her head slightly as if bringing her thoughts back from wherever they had receded.

"My parents were fine with me marrying him. His parents wouldn't hear of it because I'm half Hindu. And they wanted a proper Muslim girl for him. We married anyway. They haven't spoken to us since. But we've made it. We've kept it together for 10 years. We've moved from Atlanta to Boston to LA. Wherever life took us. And now we are here."

"What do you love about him?" I asked without meaning to.

It seemed the words just came and spilled into the glow of the flames.

"He's very handsome." Leyla joked. "He's kind. His humor. His charm. His art. He makes me feel... loved."

"You have a picture of this handsome man, Doc?" Ed asked.

Leyla scrolled through her phone and handed the phone to Ed. He took it into his massive hand.

"Wow, Doc. Movie star handsome."

Ed passed the phone to me and although I wanted to see what Raza looked like, a part of me didn't. I looked anyway, and he was perhaps one of the most striking men I had ever seen. His eyes were jovial and his smile was perfect. He seemed as tall as Leyla, but I noticed her heels in the photo and realized he must be a few inches taller if she were without shoes. He had his arm around her shoulder, his ring finger bragging a gold wedding band. Leyla was looking at him and smiling and she looked happy. She was younger in the photo and the innocence of love wrote itself across her countenance.

"That was a few months after we got married. But I love that photo of him."

I noticed how often she said 'love' when she spoke of him. I didn't want to feel anything but happiness for her but there were knots of jealousy and wistfulness within me that I just couldn't unravel. I had thought perhaps 17 years had allowed my love for her to fade but I was realizing, unwillingly but certainly, that I was in hopeless love. And now, after all this time, I could admit it, claim it, own it and yet it was still of no consequence.

Leyla's phone rang in my hand. She grabbed it and answered.

"Hello, my love," I heard her say as she got up and walked into the darkness of her office hurriedly.

"There's something not right," Ed said.

"What do you mean?"

"I've been around the block a few times, kiddo. She loves him, of that I am sure, but you see how panicked she got when the phone rang? There's something about this fella that she's not telling us."

"What Ed? That he's CIA? That he's on a mission?"

"I can't put my finger on it. And no, kiddo no CIA. I just think there's more to this guy than his art and his handsomeness."

I shrugged.

When Leyla returned from the darkness, she seemed relieved. I tried to look into her eyes but she looked away and her gaze settled onto the table.

It took me a while to realize that Leyla wasn't looking at the table but at my wrist that lay bare, proclaiming her name as it glowed in the flames of the candles.

Chapter Thirty

Tea candles rest on the rim of the tub, at the corners. Hindi love songs played from a speaker nearby as I lay in the tub with the water to my shoulders, water now tepid because I had been there for so long. I couldn't think of anything but the candlelit room, her gaze upon my wrist. I looked at her name upon me, slick with water and soft bubbles of soap. I stared then at one of the tea candles flickering gently.

The cake seemed ablaze with candles as the flames shifted with fury.

"Shut off the fan! Shut off the fan!" I said.

Prem stood watching, not shutting off the fan. His father finally did and the flames steadied, came to a lull and danced.

"Happy bird-day to you," sang the room. My parents. And his. And me. And Aasthika who mouthed the words to the song but seemed still shy as if she didn't know him very well but had been invited anyway.

He blew the candles with a single breath, had to be reminded to cut the cake. This all occurred a fortnight after the wedding. Aasthika now occupied space in the small flat and still wore stunning and dazzling sarees that her parents had sent with her. On this day she had chosen a royal blue with silver lining and streaks of silver throughout. Her bangles clinked as she divided the cake into somewhat equal pieces and her hands were still stained with henna, a deep orange.

She offered Prem a plate of cake and here his mother said, "Not like that! No, no. You must feed him. With your own hands."

Aasthika didn't answer but dutifully broke a piece of cake with her fingers, the red icing smearing across her manicured nails and held it to Prem's mouth.

He hesitated. His gaze met hers and he slowly came forward, took the piece in his mouth. As his lips singed her fingertips, his mother clapped as if this were the end of a performance. Little did she know it was the beginning of one. Or perhaps she knew but didn't want to. It is a great strength of families to ignore what is evident and to make evident that which they hope to be true. So, it was with Prem's family. And so, it would be with mine.

What saved us all from acknowledging the weight of the evening, of knowing something was off but never admitting that perhaps, perhaps it actually was, was music. I went to the massive stereo that sat by the terrace steps and turned on the sound system. I chose a CD of Bollywood love songs and adjusted the sound until it was a bit too loud. I walked back to the table. I looked from one face to the next, of everything that was unsaid but screamed in the silence. And then I ate cake.

Chapter Thirty-One

Sales at 20/20 were higher than they had ever been. I attributed it to luck and happenstance, but Sam was determined that it was Leyla who was driving sales. While I didn't believe wholly that she had turned the place around, one thing was for sure; her inclusion in 20/20 made the air different. Whereas with Dr. Bello 20/20 felt sterile and like a doctor's office, with Leyla, there was a warmth about the place that made it seem welcoming and safe. Even Ed was working more diligently, and patients seemed more at ease when they finished their exams. If more revenue was generated with Leyla's coming, it was more her presence and energy than any willful exertion on her part to make more money.

"She's fantastic," Sam beamed as he sat in his leather chair.

"She is," I said.

"Look, just look at these numbers. We might even add an extra hundred grand to this year versus last year despite Bello."

I nodded.

"I'm happy that you're happy," I said.

Sam frowned and leaned forward, his hands hitting the table with a slight thud.

"What's the matter, Priya?"

"Nothing," I said.

Nothing was the matter. Except that I missed… well I missed Leyla. The Leyla I knew. The past few months I had waited patiently for her to emerge, but she hadn't. It was as if I were living with a shell, a ghost of someone I knew. Whereas I had known her every thought, her every nuance, now I knew nothing of her and she offered nothing of herself.

I had never expected to see her again and when and if I had fantasized about the moment we met, I had imagined us as we had been, talk and laughs and tears. If we talked or laughed now, it was about a patient or about a pair of glasses. We came together at 20/20 and thereafter we went our separate ways to separate lives. It was worse than having never seen her again.

"She giving you trouble?" Sam asked.

"No" I said as I tried to extricate myself from my thoughts.

"God no. She's great."

"Then why is it that every time I talk about her this big black cloud appears over your head?"

I looked at him and wondered how to answer.

"That's not it. I just have a lot to think about, Sam."

"Oh yeah? Like what?"

"Personal, Sam."

"Priya, it's her, isn't it?"

"Sam, what could possibly upset me about Ley… Dr. Ibrahim?"

"That's what I want to know. She's on time. She works hard. The numbers are through the roof. What could possibly upset you about Dr. Ibrahim?"

"So, nothing then," I said as I got up to go to the front of the store.

"Priya?"

"Yes, Sam?"

"If there were something wrong you would tell me, wouldn't you? I mean if she weren't doing her job or if she wasn't doing the right thing?"

I sighed and wondered if Sam ever saw beyond 20/20. Did he know that not everything was tied to business? Could he even comprehend what the heart looked like?

"Priya?"

"Yes, Sam. If she weren't doing her job I would be the first person to tell you."

"But she is, right? Exams? Dilations? Recommending product?"

"Yes, Sam, she's amazing. Look at the numbers."

He seemed satisfied with the response and I left his office.

When I reached the sales floor, Ed was sitting across an Indian boy of about 15 talking to the boy's father about a pair of Nike ophthalmic frames.

"He should try them on," Ed was saying.

"Fuck you!" the boy screamed.

"Dev, is that any way to… "

"I want to go home!"

"I'm sorry." the father said looking more embarrassed than contrite.

"Just try these on for me," Ed said.

"Fuck you!" the boy repeated.

He clutched his father's arm and buried his head into it.

I slipped behind the counter and stood away from the selling station pretending that I wasn't listening and couldn't hear them. They pretended not to notice me either.

"Okay, let me take a measurement," Ed tried.

Ed withdrew his PD ruler from his shirt pocket. The boy tried to hit Ed's hand and didn't only because his father caught it in time.

"Maybe another time then," the father said.

His face had an emerging beard that was gray not because he was old but because he looked defeated. The boy looked uncomfortable. He had a slight mustache but other than that his face was bright and clear. It was his eyes though that told of the storms within him. His eyes were so troubled, I had to look elsewhere because I couldn't bear the pain within them. I wondered what tormented him.

"Let's try this again," Ed said quietly.

He picked up the frames and offered them. The boy swatted at the frames and they landed on the floor.

"This was a very bad idea." the man said. "I am sorry to have done this."

As he was about to get up, Leyla's heels sounded on the hardwood. I watched as she walked regally to the frames and picked them up. She looked at Ed and winked. It made me jealous for no reason.

"Mind if I try?" she said.

I concentrated on her crisp, clean white coat with Dr. L.M. Ibrahim scribbled in red above the pocket.

"Sure," Ed said as he got up and stood, allowing Leyla to sit.

"Hey," Leyla said.

The boy screamed.

"Hey, I just want to know your name. My name is Leyla. What is yours?"

"Dev," the boy's father answered.

Leyla put up her hand as if to tell him to stop interfering. It was a bold move.

"Hey, hi. You know I don't like people either." she said. "And all the lights in here. You want to go home, don't you? I do too. They treat you like a child, don't they? And you're not a child. You're almost a man. I know that. Don't listen to them, okay? Just relax. I'm not going to make you do anything you don't want to do."

With that Leyla spoke for 15 minutes in a gentle tone asking questions and answering them herself. I thought it was futile. I really did. But then I noticed his eyes and they seemed less troubled and more blank. His face changed, his body relaxed.

When he reached for the Nike's of his own accord, I saw Ed hold his breath.

"Can I touch the glasses?" Leyla asked.

The boy didn't respond.

"Can I check them behind your ears to see how they fit, Dev?"

A slight nod.

Her fingers touched the glasses and she was careful not to touch him. She pulled them forward a bit.

"They look great."

She showed him a mirror. He stared at his reflection as if he had never seen himself before. She gently removed he glasses, her knuckles grazing his hair. He didn't move.

"Can I measure you with a ruler?"

No response.

"Can I take a measurement with a ruler?"

Again, a slight nod.

Ed offered her his PD ruler and she took it. She held it up, close to Dev's face and took a measurement.

"That's it," she said.

She continued to speak to him and I marveled at her gentleness, her ability to calm storms. She talked for a good 20 minutes and although he didn't respond, his eyes remained blank and his body was not as tense. Ed talked to the father about lenses and suggested an identical spare pair which the father readily agreed to.

Finally, after paying and thanking Leyla profusely, the father rose and took the son's hand.

"What do you say, Dev? What do you say to the doctor?"

Dev said nothing.

"He doesn't have to say anything," Leyla said.

"Well, I will say it. Thank you so much."

"No thanks needed."

A quick handshake between the man and Leyla and then father and son walked away, Dev playing with the bells on the door before exiting.

"That is what this is about," Sam said from the corner.

None of us had realized that he had been there, listening and watching.

"Did you see that? Dr. Ibrahim, that was classic. That was great. Wow. The guy was going to walk out. You made that into a multiple sale."

Leyla said nothing, and I now watched her eyes. She looked out of the window.

"I didn't do it for your sales numbers, Sam," she said softly.

Sam looked surprised at her words.

"No, no, of course not." he said. "Just amazing how you handled that kid."

"He must have been bipolar or something," Ed said.

"They're crazy people." Sam replied. "Totally nuts."

I watched Leyla as she withdrew her gaze from the window and looked at Sam, then Ed, then me.

"What's the matter, Doc?" Ed asked.

Leyla said nothing. Her eyes were as blank as the boy's had been after the storms had passed.

When she spoke, she said, "You don't handle people. You love them."

She left us quiet in the wake of her words.

Chapter Thirty-Two

I lay awake that night trying to understand Leyla. Whenever I thought of her though, I thought of Leyla as I had known her. I couldn't think of anything I knew of her now except that she was married. She spoke to me well but as if we had just met. I looked at my phone and it was 11:36.

I quickly picked up my phone and, before I lost my nerve, I called her. One ring. Two. Three. Four.

"Hello?"

She seemed wide awake.

"Hello?"

"Priya? Are you okay?"

"I'm okay."

I tried not to breathe.

"What's the matter?"

"I'm sorry," I said.

"For what?"

"For today. If I said anything wrong. Or for not saying anything. For whatever it was that made you sad."

I felt like a fool after I said it all.

"Priya?"

"Yeah?"

I heard her sigh on the other end. I also heard soft Indian music.

"Priya, you didn't do anything wrong. But I thank you for thinking of me and calling."

Was she going to end the conversation? When there was so much I wanted to talk about. Most of all, I wanted her to talk to me like she used to. And she seemed the least bit interested in talking to me at all. I felt the sharpness of tears in my eyes and looked towards the ceiling.

"Priya?"

"Yes?"

"Rest now, okay? I'll see you tomorrow."

"Is that it?" I said more forcefully than I should have.

"Is there anything else?"

"No," I said. "Good night."

"Good night."

When she hung up and I was sure we were disconnected, I lay in my bed and wept.

Chapter Thirty-Three

"Disconnected." The card in my hand read. It was a glossy black postcard with the photo of a blurry canvas on the front. On the back, it said, "Artist Raza Ibrahim cordially invites you to an exhibit in Soho." There was a place and a time and the promise that refreshments would be served.

Leyla had walked in that morning in a flowing black skirt with swirls of red even though the weather outside was frigid even for November. She had handed each of us a card and said shyly, "Let me know if you can make it."

"So your husband really is an artist?" Ed said as he studied the card.

"He is," she said.

I watched her and my heart wished the pride she exhibited were for me. But even if the world were lopsided or convoluted and even if she were to love me and not him, I realized she would never wear that pride for me. After all, I could never imagine the question, "So your wife's an optician?" It made me feel as if my life amounted to an empty anthill while there were those who were painting colossal skies and winning full hearts.

"So, Priya, will you come?" she asked.

"Of course, I will," I said although my heart questioned whether I could handle meeting the great Raza, if indeed every constriction from the days of Jay would return and if this time I would perhaps fall apart all of my own accord.

"Great. We can go together after work that Friday. Do you think… "

"Do I think what?"

"Do you think Sam might let us leave an hour early? I mean I want to be there before it opens. I told Raza I would try."

She bit her lip in apprehension.

"Sam's got a heart, Doc." Ed said. "I think he'll let you go."

"Well, aren't you coming, Ed?" Leyla asked.

"We can't all go together. Someone's got to man the store. I'll come after I close. But I wouldn't miss it, Doc."

"You think Sam will come?"

Ed shrugged.

"No one's ever asked him to go anywhere. At least not us," Ed offered.

Leyla took my hand and the current from her fingers reached my heart.

"It's going to be great," she said.

"Is he excited?" I asked.

"Very. He's been wanting this for a long time."

"The heart wants what the heart wants," I said because that's what I always said when people spoke of love or with love and I had nothing else to say.

I went to the dispensing counter and started haphazardly checking jobs.

When Sam came in, Leyla handed him the card as soon as he entered.

"What is this?" Sam asked as he turned the card over and back.

"It's my husband's exhibit in Soho," Leyla said.

The way she said husband made me shiver just a bit. I felt the jealousy and pushed it back knowing it had no place.

"Will you come, Sam?" she asked delicately.

He looked at her and smiled.

"You know, this is the first time any of these fools have invited me to anything. Of course, I'll come. I might buy a painting."

"We were hoping to close an hour early next Friday, so we could all make it," Ed said.

There was an uncertain silence in the room. I was hoping for his business greed to overpower him. It's not that I didn't want us all to go but all this fanfare for a man none of us knew or had met started to irk me.

"An hour?" Sam said. "You know what, we can close at 5:00 instead of 7:00. Dr. Ibrahim never asks for anything and it's her big day. Her husband's big day. When he's famous, we can say we were all there."

Ed's shock was evident in the way his mouth hung just a little open.

"Thank you, Sam." Leyla said. "I can make up the time on two Saturdays if you would like."

Sam shook his head.

"See, that's what I'm talking about. That's dedication right there. I'll take you up on those two Saturdays, Dr. Ibrahim. December is going to be a killer month and I could use a little extra chair time on Saturdays."

I smiled realizing that underneath it all, it was still "about the business." But Sam had agreed to close without Leyla's offer so perhaps he did have a heart underneath it all.

I realized then that in a week and a half, I would be meeting Leyla's husband. This wasn't a college crush or a boy she liked, this was the man that had asked for her to be his for a lifetime and she had given her life to him forever.

Until then, Raza had been an idea that loomed over me. She didn't speak of him often and when she did, she never offered much information except that he wasn't feeling well (which seemed to be often, I realized) or that they had gone out to eat (which seemed to be not too often). In a week and a half, he would be real, he would have a voice and a scent and a warmth in his handshake.

I tried asking myself all the right questions, soothing myself with makeshift answers. Did it matter that she was married? No, why would it? What was I scared of, upset about? Nothing. I was scared of nothing. I wasn't upset. Why would I be? What would I say to him? Nothing. He would talk and I would respond. It wasn't like on his big night he would be paying attention to me anyway. I was just Leyla's colleague. Her colleague. Is that what I was? Yes, that's what I was. What had she said when we had first met at 20/20? "You *were* my best friend." Past tense. But it had been 17 years. Love and friendship don't stay intact if neglected over time.

I realized that no matter what I said or didn't say, I wasn't ready for the entrance of Raza Ibrahim into my life. Because the one question that loomed and lurked and had only one answer was this: Did I still love her? Yes. And yes. And yes.

Chapter Thirty-Four

The day of Raza's exhibit, there was an unusual excitement at 20/20. In all the time that we had worked together, we had never ventured anywhere save a local restaurant where Sam, Ed and I shared a dinner every Christmas. Beyond that, we had never gone anywhere and the prospect of something as novel and glamorous as an art exhibit left all of us in awe.

Leyla walked in that morning with a smile I hadn't seen her wear ever since she had started working with us. She was dressed immaculately, as usual, but carried with her a garment bag that held whatever it was she was going to wear that night. Sam has said he would meet us close to 5:00 and I assumed he would wear a designer suit with a rich colored shirt and tie. Ed, for his part, wore a shirt that actually fit and didn't gap at the belly when he sat. It was a crisp, pressed sea foam green. His tie was also longer than usual and he explained he had bought the "big and tall" variety this time. It was a swirl of colors, his tie, with hints of the same sea foam green as his shirt.

I, for my part, wore pants that were fitted rather than baggy and a black blouse with a silver trim around the neck and sheer, netted sleeves with the same silver at the cuffs. I didn't know how I looked as

Ed was the last to give a compliment or notice anything anyone wore but when Leyla had walked in that morning, she had paused and tilted her head slightly. Then, she had said slowly, "You look nice, Priya." That in itself made me feel proud and outright happy. And then, for just a moment, I wished I were the artist instead of a spectator. But the thought vanished as soon as it had risen, and we went about our day as normally as we possibly could, given the excitement that was to come in the evening.

At about 3:20, Dev came to pick up his glasses. Without hesitation, Ed went to Leyla's office and asked her to please dispense them because he was sure that if he or I were to try, it would lead to the same outcome as when Dev and his father had come in to place the order.

"How are you, Dev?" Leyla began.

"I'm good," Dev said.

He still looked worn, the father, with the same gray stubble and his hair awry. But Dev seemed different, bright and responsive.

Leyla took the glasses from the tray and held them out for Dev.

"Do you want to try the glasses on?" Leyla asked gently.

"They're cool," Dev said as he took the Nike's and put them on.

Ed and I exchanged confused looks. Was this the same Dev who had told us to fuck ourselves and screamed murder only a week ago?

"I like them," Dev said.

"You look very handsome," Leyla said as she smiled.

"And you're very pretty," Dev countered as he winked at her.

This elicited a laugh from Ed and Dev blushed as he looked away from Leyla.

"Why, thank you, Dev," Leyla said as she folded her hands and sat, judging the fit of the frames.

"Can I check the fit?" she asked.

With Dev's consent, she tugged slightly at the frames, decided they were a bit loose and heated them. Dev waited patiently, watching her. I looked at him and wondered how two worlds could coexist within him, how two such distinct people could be the same person. I wondered what had caused his outbursts and then wondered what was making him who he was as he sat there, watching Leyla.

When Leyla had adjusted the glasses and tugged at them and was satisfied with the fit, she asked, "Is that comfortable?"

"Feels great," Dev said.

"They look great," I offered.

Dev looked at his father who smiled despite his weary face.

"Let's try the second pair," Leyla said.

Dev nodded.

When Leyla was satisfied with the fit, she stepped back and smiled.

"All done," she said.

"Thank you. Let's go, Dad. I want to go play basketball."

The father rose and shook Leyla's hand.

"Some days are better than other days," he said.

"I know," Leyla said as if she knew.

With that, they left and as they exited, Dev didn't

slam on the bells, but they jangled lightly of their own accord.

"Wow. That kid is really messed up," Ed said.

Leyla turned to him.

"Why would you say that?" she asked.

"Doc, he was psycho in here last time. Did you forget?"

"We all have our demons, Ed." Leyla countered. "Sometimes we control them. Sometimes they control us. Compassion, Ed."

"I'm as compassionate as the next guy, Doc. But psycho I can't understand."

Leyla rose from her chair. Even though she was much shorter than Ed, she managed to catch his gaze and hold it before she spoke.

"Some things are better left not understood because the only way to understand them is to be in the midst of them. We don't have to understand. We just have to find enough compassion to love people through."

With that, she retreated to her office, her heels sounding desolate on the hardwood floor.

"I can't figure her out." Ed said. "It's like she doesn't see it. Like she can't admit that the guy's psycho."

I shrugged looked at the clock. It was 3:45. I started clearing the dispensing counter. I piled trays and wiped mirrors.

"I'm going out for a snack," Ed said.

"No, you're not." I said. "Because you're not going to mess up your new shirt and tie with yogurt or chocolate syrup."

He pretended to sulk but then started helping me organize and clean.

It was about half an hour later that we heard Leyla's voice behind us say, "Guys."

When we turned, we saw she had changed into her evening wear. Ed and I stopped what we were doing and we both stared as if we had never seen anyone as beautiful. Truth was, I was sure we hadn't.

In all the time that I had known her, I had only seen Leyla in a salwar kameez when we went to the temple or to the mosque. Those had been unassuming, simple clothes and even then, I had admired the way they had complemented her movements. This night, the night of the exhibit, she had chosen to wear a black and gold salwar-kameez that left Ed and me speechless. It was an ornate piece and it she made it look like it belonged on a glossy magazine page advertising some designer.

Looking at her then, my mind raced back to when the times I had seen her dress for dates or birthdays or parties. And I couldn't think of a single time she had looked as elegant or as gracious as she did now.

I thought of Raza as the face I had seen on her phone, a handsome man no doubt but I wondered if he realized how blessed, how lucky he was that her heart beat for him. Would he stop and stare at her that night as Ed and I did? Would he be speechless as we were? Because of all the things that I believed Leyla deserved, it was someone who would lose all thought upon seeing her, especially at moments like these when she seemed so perfect as to seem vulnerable.

"How do I look?" she asked in all innocence as if she really didn't know how she looked.

"You look amazing." I said. "You look amazing."

She looked to Ed who shook his head and then

said, "Sorry, Doc. Never seen a doctor as pretty as all that."

Here she laughed, and my heart constricted just a bit. I wished I didn't see in her all that I did. I wished even more and hoped, because I loved her and wanted her to know that love somehow, that Raza did.

Chapter Thirty-Five

The art gallery was a modest space with high ceilings and ample light. When we arrived, Leyla walked ahead of us, motioning for us to wait. There was still half an hour until the show began and the space, even though well-lit, seemed hollow without people. We waited by the entrance, Ed straightening his already straight tie, Sam looking at his own reflection in the glass of the door, and I feeling out of place and awkward, holding in one hand my bulky coat and letting my other hand hang at my side.

It wasn't long before Leyla returned, walking in step with Raza, holding his hand. If he had looked handsome in the photo she had showed us, he looked even more handsome in person. He wore a black suit with a stark red shirt and tie. His hair reached the nape of his neck and he had a hint of a beard. His eyes were a deep black and his smile a striking white, teeth perfectly aligned as if he were modeling for an advertisement for Colgate instead of opening an art exhibit. He was the kind of good looking movie stars are on screen except he was real life, Leyla's life I reminded myself.

"Everyone, this is Raza." Leyla beamed. "And this," she said as she held out a hand to us, "is everyone."

"Very pleased to meet you," Raza said as he shook hands with Ed and then Sam.

Then, looking at me, he smiled his Colgate smile.

"Priya. I have heard so much about you from Leyla. It is my upmost pleasure to meet you."

He let go Leyla's hand and took my hand in both of his and held it. I looked down to see our hands meet, my hand having desired Leyla, his having touched her body and mind and soul for over a decade. His hands were cool and reminded me of summer. His fingers carried the grasp of zephyrs and hot, unsettled nights. I didn't want to, but through his hands I felt the safety and the romance that she found in the nuances of his soul.

"I'm happy to meet you," I said slowly.

"The exhibit opens in about half an hour." he said. "What if I give you all a tour of the work before we open for everyone else?"

I looked at Sam who seemed out of place as, for once, he was not the one in charge. Ed gave Raza his best goofy smile. Neither of them spoke and I felt as if I had to because the silence was on the verge of awkwardness.

"We'd love that," I said.

Leyla took Raza's hand again.

"It's a small exhibit, really." He said as he started walking into the gallery. "But still, I am a bit nervous. So please, accept my humble works and let me know what you think."

We entered from the tiny foyer into a small room where Raza's art was displayed on the walls. I looked from one piece to another and felt as if his work had absorbed my angst, my love, my wistfulness and splashed it on canvas for the world to see. Each painting was unique in its colors and textures and yet each contained a small rectangle in the lower right corner where there were scribbles of red. I walked as if in a trance to one painting that was full of red in swirls with black added for depth. In the lower corner, the scribble read, "Out beyond ideas of wrongdoing and rightdoing, there is a field. I'll meet you there."

"Rumi," Raza's voice said behind me as if I didn't know.

As if one could love her and not know Rumi intimately.

"Yes," I said as I turned to face him.

"Every painting here is inspired by a verse." he said. "And I have that verse written on each painting." Then, "it began with Leyla."

I wanted to ask him what didn't begin and end with Leyla? I wanted to tell him that I knew much before he did the verses that moved her and swayed her soul and assuaged her broken heartedness. I wanted to tell him that loving Leyla made Rumi a cliché, words that seemed banal in their reciting because they were recited so often and laid so bare.

"You know there's a lot of controversy over the translations," I offered in contest.

He sighed and rubbed a gentle hand over his almost beard.

"There might be. But the verses move me as they are. They move Leyla as they are. And I use the translations. Everything worth loving is controversial, don't you think?"

Didn't I think? I thought and felt and yearned through the same verses I was now challenging. Because, truth was, he was right.

163

Divya Sood

"I want you to see my favorite," he said.

Before I could agree or disagree, he took my hand and rushed me to a canvas that was a bit smaller than the rest, the red a single stray line across, the rest of the canvas swirls of raised black and gray. The red scribble in the corner read, "In your light I learn how to love. In your beauty, how to make poems. You dance inside my chest where no one sees you but sometimes I do, and that sight becomes art."

"I call this Leyla." He said. "Of all the work here, this one is Leyla. Do you see why?"

I looked closer and through the ridges of paint, it was as if a ghost emerged. Through the gray and black and crimson, there was a faint hint of a pair of eyes. They were Leyla's eyes captured with a depth and a silence that left me in awe.

"That's amazing," I said with a tinge of jealousy.

The jealousy emerged cautiously yet it was there. Because before him, before Jay, before anyone whom she loved, had she not taught me how to love, how to write poetry? She danced inside me the moment she held a cue stick at a student center and hadn't ceased to dance since. But then, was any of that any of any consequence? Because, I reminded myself, intimacy cannot be a one-sided dance and requires a partner. Leyla had her partners and I was not and never would be one of them. This thought alone ignited the jealousy as I looked at Raza's handsomeness, his confidence, his talent.

"What's amazing is that she is in each of these paintings, Priya. Her eyes. Her smile. The way her hair falls. Look closely and you will find her."

I looked at him and he smiled and for the time he

164

held that smile I saw his gentleness and his love. I had thought that only I understood her and that only I desired her wholly without any dilution. But I realized that he did also. Difference was, and I swallowed as I realized the difference because without wanting to, my heart constricted just a bit: Leyla loved him too.

Chapter Thirty-Six

Tuesday after the exhibit, Sam had just arrived for the day and Ed was out of the office looking for a snack.

"I'm telling you, guy has a tapeworm," Sam said.

Leyla laughed at this and I tried to defend Ed.

"He needs to eat. He's a big guy," I said.

"What he needs to do is check those jobs," Sam said as he motioned with his laptop bag at the back counter.

"I can do that," I said as I walked to the lensometer.

Ed entered then with his usual frozen yogurt in one hand, a plastic spoon thrust into a pile of vanilla and strawberry yogurt, chocolate syrup threatening to spill over the rim. In his other hand, he held a newspaper.

"Look, Doc, your husband's famous!" he boomed.

Leyla looked at him in bewilderment.

"They have a piece in here about his exhibit," Ed said.

Leyla rushed to him and almost snatched the paper from his hand.

"Page 34," Ed said.

"You had time to read a paper while you got yogurt?" Sam mocked.

"I was just looking at it while I was in line." Ed said. "Read it aloud, Doc."

Leyla shuffled pages and then stopped at the page. She was glancing at the paper and her face changed from excitement to a look I couldn't decipher.

"Read it aloud," Ed insisted.

Leyla looked up and then at the paper again.

"What's wrong?" I asked.

"Raza Ibrahim's exhibit, 'For Leyla' features some compelling art which fuses the artist's unique style with ancient Sufi poetry."

"True," Sam said.

Leyla looked at him as she continued reading a few sentences. The she slowed down as she read, "Ibrahim stated that he created the exhibit for his wife, Leyla. In this day and age of extremism and terror, it is refreshing that a Muslim man can choose to create art for love."

She looked at us.

"What the hell is that?" she asked.

I was taken aback by the forcefulness of her voice.

Sam shook his head and said, "Come on, Doc. It's a great review."

"That sentence doesn't bother you?"

Sam shrugged.

"It's a newspaper. They're bound to be political."

"It's the arts section, Sam. The arts section."

"Doc, you can't let that get to you," Ed offered.

Leyla threw the paper down on the selling station desk.

"Can't let that get to me? That my husband is an artist. A lover. And someone sitting at a desk decided that he "chose" art? Chose it over what? Raza didn't choose art over anything. Art chose him and gave him this talent, this gift. And if he weren't a 'Muslim man,' then this wouldn't even be a suggestion. That he chose art over what?"

I looked from Sam to Ed. Sam was fiddling with his laptop bag and Ed was concentrating on the yogurt he was trying carefully not to spill onto his shirt. I slowly looked at Leyla and she looked flushed, angry, pained.

"It's a good review," I tried.

"I don't expect any of you to understand," she finally said. She turned, and her heels sounded hollow as she walked to her office and shut the door.

"Wow." Ed said, "She's really angry."

I was still smarting from her words. She didn't expect any of us to understand? Including me? But then what did I really understand? I understood she was angry. I also understood that the review was positive, touting the art as "brilliant." How a string of words, one line in that article had so infuriated her, I understood that also. But, even though I didn't want to admit it, if she hadn't pointed out the line, I would have missed it completely taking no umbrage to the words, glossing over them. That perhaps was my failing. So perhaps I didn't really understand.

"Do something," Sam said.

"What do you want me to do?" I asked.

"I don't know. She can't be like that all day."

"Are you worried about your numbers or about her, Sam?" I shot back.

"Easy, kiddo." Ed said. "You know we love Doc. We're worried about her."

"Try to talk to her, please," Sam said.

I walked to the office door and knocked lightly. There was no answer.

"Leyla?"

"Is there a patient?"

"No. Just wanted to know if you would like some lunch maybe?"

"No," was the reply.

I stood waiting for her to open the door for me.

I waited a long time.

She didn't open the door. I kept waiting. When she finally opened the door to walk to the bathroom, she was startled.

"Priya? Have you been standing here this whole time?" she asked.

"No," I lied. "Just passing by."

Chapter Thirty-Seven

Passersby couldn't help but notice the garlands of flowers that streamed from the windows and balcony of the flat. I myself had paused before entering when I had arrived the day before. And then, upon entering, I had been accosted with sweets of all sorts. It was a few days after a year of the wedding. And, as if on cue for a script, Aasthika had given birth to a baby boy.

I had found out by way of a jarring awakening one night. One night close to a week ago while I had tossed and turned and thought of nothing and everything and had almost slept, the phone had rung.

"Priya!"

"Prem, how are you?"

"She—I mean Aasthika—it's a boy."

"Congratulations," is what I said.

"Thank you." Was all he answered.

There was silence.

"Can you come here for a bit?"

He asked as if he lived next door, as if "a bit" didn't involve a journey that spanned thousands of miles. But regardless, I would go. I didn't know then that it would be the last visit where I saw him, where I should have saved him somehow from himself. I didn't know what brewed within him for the entire visit was short, a week because that's all the time I could afford. This was all before 20/20, before Leyla's resurgence, before the life I lived now. And still, if I think of it, I am there, immersed in what transpired and what was and wasn't and the lives of those I would not know again.

The week was filled with people and color and smells of happiness. Tea was constantly on the stove, milk boiling, sugar added for the many who stopped by, who marveled at how efficiently Aasthika had produced a son. Paper bags brimmed with fresh samosas that were served with tea and sweets—rosogollas and panthuas and mishit doi—were readily available any time of day or evening.

Prem smiled a lot, held his son with affection, placed lingering kisses upon his head. He placed his hand on his son's chest, his fingers broad and wide and big. But in his eyes, the same vacuous look, the same emptiness I had seen for so long. I started to believe that there was no vacancy in his eyes because it was easier than to believe that there were gaps in his soul that were gaping and raw.

"He's beautiful," I said as I teased the baby's tightly wound fist with my forefinger.

Prem merely smiled at me without speaking.

We never spoke at length during that trip. There were no games of Campa Cola. There were no conversations in the makeshift temple. It seemed things had changed and yet I didn't know what. I tried to believe he was a family man now, that regardless of the twists and turns he had endured to get there, he was now, to use the word of the aunties, "settled" in life.

I didn't know then that he couldn't settle for the restlessness inside him. I didn't know that when I left him, it would be to his thoughts and demons and a few feet of rope.

Chapter Thirty-Eight

Life at 20/20 after the exhibit ran just as it did before except Sam and Ed were in awe of Raza and made it known. They asked Leyla often about her "artist husband" and Leyla sometimes blushed and smiled yet sometimes held a distant look in her hazel eyes that none of us could decipher. Sam for his part had bought a painting at the exhibit and hung it proudly over the patient chairs outside the doctor's office. It was a beautiful piece with the red scribble, "Let yourself be silently drawn by the strange pull of what you really love. It will not lead you astray."

Sam joked (although I believed he was semi-serious) when he said he bought it because he wanted us to be inspired to be pulled into "the business."

"It's a strange love, optical." Sam had mused after two drinks at the restaurant Raza had taken us to after the exhibit. "But it is a love. A passion. A desire. It's not just a business. It sucks you in, Raza."

Raza had smiled his Colgate smile and nodded. I, for my part, had wanted to ask Raza where Leyla was in the painting because beyond striking crimson on the canvas, I couldn't discern her eyes or her falling hair. But I didn't ask, emboldened as I was after two drinks myself.

"20/20 is your love," I said instead to Sam who quickly responded, "Who needs a mistress when the love of his life is so full of life?"

We had laughed at that. We had had a pleasant dinner with even Ed making jokes. Leyla had been sitting next to Raza and by the end of the evening, whether she was tired or whether she was just being affectionate I didn't know but she was leaning on his shoulder, her hand grazing his arm.

I was admiring the painting, looking for Leyla in the swirls and lines of paint when the door jangled. I turned to see two young girls walk in, probably in their mid-20s, holding hands. When they looked at each other, it was as if they made the room and the world dissolve around them. When they exchanged a slight kiss on the lips, I looked away, embarrassed, then looked around to see if anyone else had seen. It was as if they held my secret out in the open and I felt that if anyone saw, they would know that I too yearned for this intimacy, this closeness with another.

"Can I get an eye exam here?" one of them asked.

"Sure." I said. "Insurance?"

"No," she said.

The one who had asked had striking auburn hair and blue eyes. The one that held her hand had black hair, same as mine and brown eyes a shade darker. She looked Indian to me, but I wasn't sure. I fumbled as I found blank paperwork for the one getting an exam. I handed her the clipboard shakily.

"You can have a seat in one of the chairs there," I said gesturing to the chairs in front of the doctor's office.

They walked to the chairs and sat, giggling and touching throughout the time it took the girl to fill out

173

the forms. When they handed the forms back to me, I arranged the paperwork, slid it into a folder and walked to Leyla's office.

"We have a walk-in," I said.

She took the file from me and her eyes met mine.

"You okay?" she asked.

"Yes, why wouldn't I be?"

"Don't know. Seem jittery."

I walked off without answering her and ushered the girl into the exam room.

"Can I go too?" her girlfriend asked.

"Sure," Leyla said from the door as she smiled at them.

I waited for the exam to finish and felt the tension in my shoulders and back.

"Hey kiddo, I got my free yogurt today," I heard Ed say as he walked through the door.

He sounded far away, everything seemed as if I were under water as I thought of having to help the couple in the exam room.

"I filled up my card and they really do give you the 11th one free," Ed continued.

I watched him spoon yogurt and chocolate syrup into his mouth and was envious of his oblivion, of his ability to be happy with the small things.

"Don't tell Sam but I'm going to eat this in his office. Just five minutes."

"Sure," I said.

Ed walked to the back, his gait lopsided and uneven making him seem like a child when he walked. I watched him until he entered Sam's office and then waited for Leyla to finish the exam. When Leyla finally emerged, she was laughing and smiling, talking to the

174

girls about the importance of sun protection. She walked to me and handed me the file.

"Nicole definitely needs glasses for distance and the computer. And we were talking about a pair of dedicated sunglasses for her trip to the Dominican Republic next month. Lots of sun. Coming to think of it, Jasmine should also have a pair of sunglasses to put over her contacts as well." Then, "Priya's great. She'll make sure you get something you love."

I leafed through the file pretending to read it or look for something when, in actuality, there was nothing for me to look for.

"What style do you like?" I asked Nicole.

"What style do I like, babe?" she asked Jasmine.

They laughed and then chose frame after frame, smiling at the ones that they liked, frowning at the ones they didn't. There were only two frames where they disagreed; the rest got a smile or a frown from both of them. I marveled at how in tune they were with each other, how the synchronicity of their likes, their dislikes, their very being was evident.

"You must hate us by now," Jasmine said.

"No." I said. "Not at all."

"How do you do this all day?" she asked.

I smiled without meaning to.

"You get used to it."

"Babe, what about these?" Jasmine asked as she slipped on a pair of Jimmy Choo sunglasses.

"I love them!"

"Should I get these?"

"Absolutely."

I thought perhaps the price tag would deter them from the sunglasses, but it didn't.

"I like these and these," Nicole said as she tried on a Prada sunglass and then a Tom Ford ophthalmic.

"They're both nice," I suggested.

"They're perfect," Jasmine said.

With the frames settled, it was time for lenses.

"So we have many different lenses," I started.

It was an easy sale as Nicole had a proclivity for the best and Jasmine wholeheartedly agreed that the best was indeed the best option. As I explained lens features, I noticed them holding hands. I was in awe of their mere togetherness, their understanding for and of each other. I tried to focus on lenses, but my thoughts swam in oceans of wonder at the genesis of relationships. I wondered at what moment the heart jumped and said, "You're it." As if in surprise, in a hide and seek game of tag.

I had had one relationship in my entire life, five years after college, a clandestine affair that seemed like it would do. She had said she loved me and I believed she had but my reticence, my embarrassment regarding the whole affair had frustrated her. She had tried coaxing me out of my fears, even gone as far as to place a ring on my finger. When that hadn't worked, she had left slowly, slipped away almost and I hadn't stopped her because I knew that my heart didn't beat for her but saw her just as enough, as someone not to love but to hold onto. It wasn't fair because I knew she saw me as so much more.

"So, what's the damage?" Nicole asked as I stole a glance at my naked ring finger.

When I relayed their total, they both laughed and looked at each other.

"Wow. That's more than the cost of our trip," Jasmine said.

Nicole pulled out a credit card and handed it to me with no hesitation.

After Nicole signed the receipt and I thanked them both, I sat and tried to think of nothing at all. As they exited, and bells jangled, Leyla walked out of her office and stood in front of me.

"How was the sale?"

"It was great," I said with as much enthusiasm as I could muster.

"They're a sweet couple." Leyla said. "In the exam room they were really great. Really in love it seems."

I nodded. I was uncomfortable. What if Leyla knew I had imagined myself as half that couple and her as the other half? What if she knew that although I tried to banish these thoughts, they still rose, despite Raza, despite 17 years of rumination?

"You, my dear, have to find someone to love," Leyla said.

"Do you wish me love like you have with Raza?"

I didn't know how the question surfaced or how it so quickly was spoken but I had said it and it hung in the air.

"Do not be satisfied with the stories that come before you." she said as she smiled slightly. "Don't live someone else's love story, Priya. Create your own."

"How?" I asked softly.

"For one," she answered as her hand grazed my cheek, "stop loving me as you do."

Chapter Thirty-Nine

Sam decided that the Christmas party would be at a fancy Manhattan restaurant. For three years Sam, Ed, and I had shared a quiet meal at a decent restaurant in Jackson Heights. But this year, Sam had said that he wanted to do something special for us, something different. He asked often about whether we were free the next Saturday, the weekend before Christmas, and also asked Leyla just as often if Raza would be able to make it.

"We'd love for him to join us," he said one Tuesday afternoon after a rush of patients had left and it was just Ed, Leyla, Sam and me.

"He'd love that," Leyla said.

"Well good, then it's settled. We're going to have a great time." Then, looking at me, "Priya, office?"

"Sure," I said as I smiled at him.

We still met weekly and he still wanted more, always wanted more than what we were doing but ever since Leyla had joined us, he seemed more relaxed and reassured. Instead of in-depth conversations about the business, our time in the office became a quick assessment of profit, Sam's unending praise of Leyla and then a languid conversation about the weather or a patient anecdote. That day was no different.

"Priya, she's credentialed with the big companies now," Sam started.

"And we're seeing more people because of it."

"Exactly. She's amazing."

"She is."

"Just one thing. One thing I wanted to ask you."

I waited as his eyes shifted from me to the wall behind me. It seemed whatever he wanted to ask needed to be asked but was also something he didn't want to ask.

"What's that?"

"Nothing. Never mind."

"Tell me Sam. Almost four years and you've told me everything. I think. So, tell me this too."

He took a deep breath and released it slowly.

"Do you see that sometimes she just seems out of it? I mean she does her work really well. But sometimes, do you notice she seems, I don't know, sad?"

I had noticed but I hadn't realized that Sam had noticed.

I shrugged.

"Maybe she has off days."

"Maybe. But I like her, Priya. You don't think she's upset about the job?"

"Sam, I really don't think it's 'the business' that gets her like that."

"Then what do you think it is?"

"I don't know."

As we sat and surmised as to Leyla's moods, there was a knock on the door.

"Come in," Sam said.

Leyla opened the door gently and stood in the doorway without a word.

"Dr. Ibrahim. Did you need something?"

"I—I was wondering, I mean I know it's been busy but could I possibly leave?"

"Leave?" Sam asked as if in disbelief.

"Yes, you see Raza is not well and I really have to be home."

Sam sat up and placed his hands on the table.

"Well, if it's illness, then of course, Dr. Ibrahim."

Before he could continue, she was gone, the door slightly open, Sam and I exchanging puzzled looks.

"Do you think it has anything to do with Raza?" Sam asked. "Maybe she's unhappy?"

"Seems happy." I said. "Sam, I should get out front."

Truth was, I couldn't discuss Leyla as if she wasn't the Leyla I loved. Sam's conversation was making me anxious and I didn't want him to see that. The more he spoke, the worse I felt and the more I thought of instances where her smile had faded, or she had looked weary. But then I had attributed it to being tired. But what if something was genuinely wrong? But what could I do? How could I even know?

"Give me a few minutes." He said. "It's going to be quiet out there anyway with no doctor."

"What is it, Sam? Why are you analyzing her?"

I knew I sounded more defensive than I should have.

"I'm not *analyzing* her. I'm just wondering. I like her, Priya. I just wish if there was anything she needed from me..."

"She needed to go home, and you were nice about it."

"True."

"Hey Sam," Ed bellowed from the hallway.

I rose thinking there was a patient that needing help.

"Doc forgot her phone." Ed said. "She ran out of here so fast. It was ringing after she left. I found it in her office."

"She probably doesn't even realize she left it," Sam said.

"I can go give it to her after work," I offered not knowing where Leyla lived.

I don't know why I offered. It wasn't as if Leyla and I had ever met or spoken outside of 20/20 save the exhibit.

"Would you?" Sam asked. "I'm sure she'll need it. I can call her and tell her you'll take it over. I'll give you the address."

"Sure," I said.

I didn't know I was about to unravel another story in the chapters of Leyla's life.

Chapter Forty

The address Sam gave me for Leyla was in Manhattan. I didn't know why I had never thought to ask her where she lived or why I had assumed she lived somewhere in Queens. I took the train to Fifth Avenue and walked the 15 blocks and two avenues to her building. I had had her phone in my coat pocket and I touched it from time to time to make sure it was still there.

As I neared her building a slight panic built inside me. I didn't know why but I was nervous, feeling as if I were intruding into her life. It angered me that at one point in our lives, coming and going from apartment to dorm room hadn't fazed us. We had seamlessly slid in and out of every aspect of our lives, our habitation, or habits. And then there were those 17 years that forged a gaping hole between us so now I was afraid to even step foot across the threshold of her apartment.

When I reached the building, the doorman asked where I was going.

"Seventeenth floor." I said. "Ibrahim."

"Are they expecting you?"

"Yes." I said.

He nodded, and I took the elevator up, fixing my coat and my hair as I stared at my reflection in the mirror that formed when the doors closed. When I reached the apartment, I contemplated knocking or ringing the bell. I rang the bell. With the sound of the buzz, I was taken back suddenly and slightly to a buzzer that had changed our lives, first when she had pressed it to make an excuse to talk to Jay and second when I had pressed it and gone up to see him.

"Priya," she said as she opened the door.

"Who is it?" Raza asked from inside.

His voice was his but it was also not his. It was deeper, sleepier and yet more disturbed in some ways than when he had spoken at the gallery.

"Priya," Leyla said.

"Tell her to come in. Or doesn't she want to see me?"

Again, the voice was different. The confidence he had exuded at the exhibit seemed lost and in its place, there was a slight agitation, a slight insecurity that I couldn't place within him.

"Come in," Leyla said hesitatingly.

"Here's your phone," I said as I pulled her phone out of my pocket.

She took it in her hand, looked down at it absentmindedly.

"Please come in," she said in a way that sounded weary and defeated.

When I entered the apartment, I stood at the entrance marveling at the splendor of it all. It was a simple space but tasteful, Raza's paintings hung thoughtfully on the walls, track lighting accenting just the right places. Leyla led me through a small foyer to the living room. As I looked around, my gaze stopped when I saw Raza on the couch, swaddled in a blanket. He was sitting up and staring at a TV that was off. If

Leyla had said he was unwell, he looked unwell. But he didn't look sick either.

"How are you feeling?" I asked as I was not sure what to say.

His eyes turned to me and I saw that his beard was now full and untamed.

"What did Leyla tell you? That her crazy husband needs her? That's what she told you when she left work?"

Confusion clouded my mind. It seemed I didn't know this man who weeks ago had been pristine, confident, the artist that left even Sam in awe. In place of that Raza, the man on the couch was unkempt and his eyes were devoid of the exuberance they had held at the gallery.

"I'm sorry?" was all I could muster.

"Don't lie to me!" he screamed.

"Baby, I never said those things. I promise," Leyla said as she sat beside him.

Tenderly and gingerly she took his hand and said his name.

"Listen to me." she said. "You've had a long day. Why don't you take your medicine and try to sleep? Would you like that?"

I didn't quite understand the scene. My mind replayed Leyla in her salwar kameez, radiant and proud. I thought to the crispness of Raza's red shirt. And then this, him swaddled in a blanket, her speaking to him as if to a child. Both seemed tired. Both seemed defeated by a force I didn't know but could feel.

"Don't tell me what to do," Raza said a bit too loudly.

"I think I should go," I said even before I sat.

There was silence. In that silence, all I discerned was my own heartbeat and a palpable despair which filled the room. Finally, Raza looked at me, but the emptiness of his eyes made me look away.

"You can stay." he said softly. "I'll go. I'm going to bed."

He rose abruptly, went to the kitchen. I heard the tap as he turned it on, shut it off. Then he returned and bent to kiss the top of Leyla's head.

"I love you a lot, Leyla." he said in Urdu.

His accent was a slight fault of the lilt of his tongue, a sweet grazing of words. He said her name like a prayer, half a whisper when I thought I was the only one who could do that. But I wasn't. He shared an intimacy with her that I had never known, and it puzzled me because it was an intimacy that contained both the quick trots of happiness and the slow waltzes of pain. Both were evident in the way he touched her forehead to push her hair back and to place a final kiss before he left. After, Leyla motioned for me to sit next to her and I did, waiting for her to speak.

"My husband," she began.

She cleared her throat. Swallowed.

"Thing is, thing is, he's an amazing artist. An amazing man. Thing is. Thing is he has this, this, he suffers. A lot."

"I don't understand," I said bluntly.

"He has bipolar disorder," she finally said as if the words were difficult in and of themselves.

It sounded like a confession.

"What does that mean?" I asked.

I had heard the term but mostly when a patient was difficult, like Dev had been, and Ed or Sam had

185

thrown the word to describe the patient. I never had had to stop to wonder what it meant. And I honestly didn't know.

"He's two people in one, kind of," she said as she tried to smile. "Some weeks are good weeks and he paints and writes and his art and me, that's all he needs. Some weeks nothing is enough, and I am afraid of his sadness, his inertia. I'm scared he'll hurt himself. Or have an episode of some sort. This week is one of those weeks."

I sat dumbfounded trying to grapple with what she had said and also wondered how difficult it must be to love him.

"But you love him?" I asked. "Even when he's— he's like that?" I asked.

It wasn't the most sophisticated way to ask the question, but I was at a loss for finesse.

"Of course, I love him. Priya. Love doesn't promise an easy ride. That doesn't mean you stop loving."

"But I mean how do you know which person he'll be?"

She took my hand and played with my fingers.

"I don't. Day to day I don't. But in the beginning, at first, there was the temper. Between the happiness and the sadness there was the anger. And with the medicine he takes, a lot of that is controlled. It's better. It's just… I wish I could help him more than love him."

"It's not fair," was all I could think of to say.

"Mostly to him," she said.

"So now what?" I asked.

"So now? Now nothing," she said as she looked

into my eyes.

I had to look away because when she looked at me like that, all that rose within me was desire for her. It felt selfish and it felt egotistical, desiring her when she was dealing with the madness of the desire of her life.

"I didn't know," I said because I didn't know.

"I know. I don't tell anyone. I mean, we told his parents and they blamed me, said it was me who was driving him mad. It was a terrible time. That's why we moved to New York. But sometimes I wonder if it is me, if I make him worse."

"It's not you," I insisted.

She sat quietly still playing with my hand. I didn't know what to offer as an antidote to her pain. I wondered how she could survive not knowing who she would wake up next to, Raza the artist or Raza as he was now.

"Is that why you're sad sometimes?" I asked. "Is that why you keep checking your phone, to see if he is okay?"

She looked at me and I saw she had tears she was trying desperately not to let fall.

"What can I do, Priya?" she asked. "Except be there for him. Love him. Hope. And hope. And hope."

Chapter Forty-One

"Hope is the thing with feathers that perches in the soul." Emily Dickinson wrote that. I remember analyzing the rhythm of it in a college literature class a long time ago. I remember relating it, as I related everything back then, to Leyla, to hope that had no cause nor rhyme nor rhythm. I think now of Prem with hope, always, that he is happy and fulfilled and full of the life that seemed to have seeped from his eyes in the past few years.

The summer was stagnant save a slow, warm breeze that teased the leaves outside the window. It was the last day I would speak to him not that week nor that month nor this year but ever. Ever. What a finality and we never know when the last of anything occurs until it is over with, done, finitely sealed into the past.

It is he who called me. He called me, and I picked up instantly. He was happy or sounded happy or pretended he was happy, I still don't know which.

"How are you?" I asked.

"I am well, Priya. I am well."

I didn't know then that "well" meant "well until I hang myself to death in a month leaving a wake of emptiness and confusion, many questions unanswered and many answers one wants to acknowledge.

"Good. I am well also."

"How is your work?"

"I enjoy it."

"Plans to come to Calcutta?"

"Soon," I said although I had no plans.

We talked of how we hadn't seen each other since the baby's birth, how we hadn't talked since he had called after the naming ceremony and proclaimed, "Abhaijeet... that is my son's name. Brave. And fearless." He never stated, "Unlike me" but it was a comment inherent in his words although I found him plenty brave and very fearless having embraced a life that wasn't of his choosing. We didn't mention Aasthika although she was inhabiting his space and his life. We spoke of banal things, the weather and new Bollywood movies and how big Abhaijeet was becoming. It seemed as though those days of thatched mats and temple talks were far behind us, perhaps as if they had never existed.

I never addressed the guilt that rose within me for having lost touch, for not doing my part to keep alive nights of talking and Campa Cola games. I never explained why my phone calls were fewer and fewer until they were lost in silence. It was as if on the day he had married I had let him go, let him swim alone in an ocean of unfamiliarity.

"How is the coffee shop?" I asked.

"It's great. We're renovating."

I should have known by the word "great" that nothing was. I should have called his bluff, known his intentions. He was, after all, calling not to say "hello" as I thought but "goodbye" as I know now.

I am afraid of forgetting his voice. As silly as that seems, that is perhaps my greatest fear, to never be able to conjure his voice in my head. I know I will never lose

189

the image of him. There are photographs for things like that. But his voice, his mannerisms, his laughter rare but present. These are the things I fear forgetting.

Although, on that day we talked last, I thought none of this. I thought none of this because I had no way of knowing that it was a last that I would endure for the rest of my life.

Chapter Forty-Two

The day of the Christmas party, Sam was in an exceptional mood. He had come to 20/20 early despite it being a Saturday and was watching the flow of patients that were streaming in to use their end of year insurance and flex spending benefits. Ed and I were trying to finish sales quickly as we didn't even have time to get up from our chairs before one patient left and another sat.

I watched Leyla from time to time and when she caught my eye she smiled or winked as she traveled to and from the examination room. I looked at Sam who was debating whether to help us sell or watch us sell. He got some insane pleasure out of watching the process without actually being a part of it whereas I always got a thrill from being a part of the process, watching the totals add up, watching the numbers rise.

Although we closed at 6:00, we were well past 7:00 when the last patient left, the bells jangling brightly as the door closed and Ed ran to lock it.

"That's enough," he said, and I laughed.

"What a day!" Sam said.

He was leaning back in one of the dispensing chairs, his hands clasped behind his head. His eyes were sparkling as they did when he saw 20/20 sparkle and flourish. It was his one true love, "the business" and he treated it as such.

Leyla came from her office and said, "I am so tired."

"You can't be tired, Doc," Ed said. "Dinner tonight."

Leyla looked at me as she spoke.

"I won't be able to make it."

"Why not, Doc?"

"Raza is a bit under the weather," she said.

She didn't stop looking at me as if waiting for me to say something, to betray her. Or to betray Raza. She knew I would do neither.

"Maybe we should reschedule," I offered.

"You don't have to do that," Leyla said.

"Well if you aren't feeling up to it." Sam said.

Leyla looked from me to Sam and back at me.

"Reschedule then," she said decidedly and then walked to her office to collect her things.

Sam sat back in his chair and Ed cleared his throat.

"He's always under the weather." Ed said. "Guy needs some Vitamin C or something."

"Well, it is what it is." Sam said as he stared towards the examination room.

"Ed, close out, will you?" I said as I walked to Leyla's office.

"Are you okay?" I asked as I shut the door behind me.

She sat heavily in the examination chair. She looked small in the chair.

"Sometimes I just can't." she said. "Like last night. He was so out of it. He was paranoid and crying asking me if I would rather just be with someone else.

He accused me of seeing someone. Priya, I can't do this anymore. I feel so… alone. I mean, he has me. Who do I have to talk to?"

I looked at her eyes becoming moist and glistening with her pain and fear. I couldn't see her like that. I thought back to nights when she had cried with me, her head on my shoulder for things that were sometimes warranting of that grief and sometimes not. But I had been there. And, I decided, I would be there again in any way I knew how.

"You can talk to me," I said slowly.

She smiled slightly.

"I always could." she said. Then, "Is that fair to you though?"

I had never thought of my time with Leyla as fair or unfair. Love, in all its stickiness and its many dimensions was not fair. Love demanded more than it ever gave, and sometimes rendered us powerless in its grip. Leyla was the love I knew and the only love I had ever known. But I also knew that I loved Leyla because it was easy loving Leyla. It was a love based in worship, of admiring from afar without fear and I knew that those whom we worship cannot hurt us. It is a one-sided love based in faith. And that is how I loved her. The way she loved Raza, that was a different love, a love that asked and gave and took. It was the acceptance of a soul, however flawed or imperfect. I had never been ready to let go and to love like that. And I wasn't ready still. And so, I offered myself to her, as I always had, because worship was all I had ever known.

"Why wouldn't it be?" I said finally. "I was your best friend."

"Will you come home with me?" she asked. "He likes you. He trusts you. It's not logical; he barely knows you. But he is comfortable with you. And I... I need you."

That is all she had to say. She was asking, once again, for me to enter her in the same way I had so long ago. And I knew it had almost destroyed me then, that one-sided dance had left me tired and unable to create any other movement in my life. But as I looked at her tiredness, her desperation, I couldn't hold back, couldn't stay just someone she knew at 20/20. History has a force that is stronger than the present moment, all tenses are not created equal. And, if I had been there for her then, I would be there for her again. All I knew at the moment was this: Leyla needed me, and I was grateful.

Chapter Forty-Three

When we entered the doorway, Leyla turning the key and me behind her, the stale smell of cigarette smoke lingered in the air. I remembered her removing a cigarette from my mouth so many years ago and looked at her questioningly. It was as if she understood the question my eyes held and said softly, "He smokes sometimes. Not all the time. But when he's really down, he smokes a lot."

"And you're okay with that?"

"Priya, it's the least of my worries."

She closed the door behind me and said forcefully and cheerfully, "I'm home, babe. And guess who decided to visit?"

We walked into the living room where Raza sat on the couch, swaddled in the same blanket I had seen him in the last time, rocking himself back and forth on the couch. I remembered for an instant my cousin who had the same habit of rocking when he sat and was disturbed and was flooded with a need to speak to him although I knew I couldn't and would never. The thought left as quickly as it had come and yet I thought of him again and wondered as to his grief and demons and then, looking at Raza, wondered as to his mind. Their lives were different, their griefs different yet they shared a desperation. Difference was, my cousin didn't have a lover's voice or hands to soothe him. Had he had someone who had found him and loved him, would he be alive? And if Raza had not had Leyla, would he be dead?

"Priya," Raza said sleepily and so interrupted my thoughts.

"Hey," I said.

Leyla sat next to him and took his hand. She motioned for me to sit in an armchair across and I did.

"I'm not at my best," Raza said as he kept his gaze upon me.

I looked into his eyes and they were just as vacuous as they had been the last time, his beard about the same length and just as unkempt. I broke eye contact with him because I felt as if I would get lost in the sad caverns of his eyes and never return to myself. I looked about the room and focused on a photo of Raza and Leyla where he was the radiant, charming Raza I had first met. Leyla said he went back and forth between the confident artist and not. I wondered when the artist would return. I wondered how she lived not knowing and hoping every minute of every day that her love would heal him.

"How are you?" I asked as I kept looking at the photograph.

"I'm okay." he said. "Thank you for asking."

"Babe, did you eat?"

"I did. I went and got some Chinese."

"You shouldn't go out when you don't feel well," Leyla said and, upon hearing the alarm in her voice, I looked at her.

"Why?" I asked without meaning to.

Leyla shot me a look that stopped me from asking again. Raza said nothing.

"Let's watch a movie," Leyla suggested.

I said nothing as I was afraid of saying the wrong thing.

"You guys watch." Raza said. "I'm going to take some meds and go to bed. I don't feel up to it."

It was only after I heard him in the kitchen running the tap that I spoke.

"I'm sorry," I stumbled.

"No, I'm sorry." Leyla said as she looked up at the ceiling. "I'm sorry. The thing is, if he goes out like this and he gets upset, he can get hurt. It happened once. He got into an argument over an apple."

"An apple?" I asked not sure I understood.

Actually, I didn't understand at all.

"He went to the store and picked up an apple. He bit into it and the guy who was stocking the apples told him he couldn't do that. So, Raza got angry and started screaming. Then he started getting paranoid and accusing the guy of all these things and they finally restrained him, and he ended up handcuffed. I had to leave work and go to the police station. This was in Atlanta. At Kroger's."

"Was he okay? I mean when you went to get him?"

"Priya, I'm lucky they didn't attack him or shoot him. The thing is, they see his face, they read his name before they see his mind. They don't assume he's unwell or disturbed. They assume he's dangerous. That's why I get scared, Priya. I don't want them to hurt him or kill him."

"You don't think you're being dramatic?"

"Do you live under a rock, Priya? Do you look around you? Do you read the news?"

"Sorry."

"No, I'm sorry. Just... I'm sorry."

We sat silently and I reluctantly admitted to myself that I regretted coming. It was as if I didn't have the correct answer to any question on the test of friendship or of love that was placed before me. Whereas back then I knew the nuance of every one of her thoughts and moods and emotions, now, I knew nothing of what she thought or felt or how or why. I wanted to help her, but she seemed in a world I couldn't understand nor enter.

"Priya, I'm sorry. Let's have a pleasant evening. No more talk of this."

I shrugged and tried to shrug off my hurt as well.

Raza came from the kitchen holding a bottle of wine and some glasses.

"Let's have some wine." he said, "Before I go to bed."

"You're not supposed to drink with the medications," Leyla said flatly.

He ignored her and set the glasses on the glass table and poured. I noticed he poured less in one glass than the other two.

"I'll have just this much," he said as he smiled at her.

In that smile, the artist emerged, and his eyes flickered with gentleness. In that smile was the man that had captured her heart, the man I had met and admired, and she adored. I looked at her and knew she wouldn't give him a hard time about the wine.

"Just that much," she said softly.

198

"A toast," he said.

"A toast?" Leyla asked.

"To Priya. For her courage to come here and encounter the madness."

He laughed slightly after and I looked at Leyla who looked more at peace than she had earlier.

"Priya, it's nice of you to be here with us," he said.

A clinking of glasses. Sips of wine.

Raza set down his glass and walked to the other end of the room. He returned with a leather journal and handed it to Leyla.

"Today, I wrote," he said as he sat next to Leyla on the couch.

She took the book from him and smiled. It was a smile that lit up her eyes so that they were hopeful and beautiful just for an instant.

"Thank you, my love. Can I read this to Priya?"

Raza contemplated as he rubbed his beard. He drank some more wine.

"You can. But after I go to bed."

Leyla leaned into him and kissed him gently on the lips. There was a connection between them that was palpable, an understanding, a non-spoken covenant of love. It was unlike anything I had known. As I looked at them, I felt as if I were spying on them, leering at the most private minutes of their lives. As I watched him watch her, I saw the vacuousness of his eyes fill with her and he drank her in as I had done so many times. Difference was, she drank from his eyes as well and nourished her heart and soon she was laughing and he was laughing and I felt as if I should evaporate and leave them be. But then Raza started telling me stories and I joined their night, their laughter and realized how warm and whole their world was. Did every love that was requited feel so whole? I didn't know and I started to realize I wanted to. For the first time in my life, I wasn't just jealous of the person Leyla loved. I was jealous also of the way she was loved back.

Chapter Forty-Four

After Raza went to bed, Leyla sat with the journal in her lap. She looked at me and smiled and looked happy after a long time.

"Back when we first got married, about a year into our marriage, that's when Raza started acting differently. He had days he was full of energy and he'd paint all night. I thought he was just inspired. But then he would have days where he was just grumpy and angry, and every little thing angered him. And then there were days he was miserable, and he slept most of the time or lay on the couch. I thought maybe the marriage had changed him. I thought I had made him moody or upset. And then one day he was on a real high and he swore he could fly out the window. He opened it and I had to fight with him, restrain him and I knew something was definitely wrong."

"He wanted to fly out of a window?" I asked.

I still didn't understand most of what she said when it came to Raza.

"He did. He seriously did. And after we spent the night fighting about it, I talked him into seeing a doctor at a nearby hospital. And they talked to him and it took a month or so but they diagnosed him as bipolar."

"And then?" I asked.

"And then and then and then." She said as she smiled wearily. "And then the medications they tried didn't work. For months. And the ups and downs and the anger. For months. But it was during that time that he came to me one night and sat on the edge of the bed and just cried. And he said, 'I can't tell you sometimes. Or anymore.'

'I held him for a long time. And then he handed me a journal and said, 'I write for you everything that I can't say. I am scared every minute of every day that I will lose you.'

'Priya, I had thought about leaving, about finding an easier person to be with. I did. But once I read his words, once I saw how he loved me, I resolved to love him through. The love I searched for my whole life found me. I was used to running away, to finding easier ways. To this day, he fills journals for me."

"Can you read some of it?" I asked curious as to how his words had moved her to love him whereas any words I had ever written had gotten nods and slight praise but never her love.

She opened the journal to the very beginning, to the fresh start before the pages began just inside the cover.

"I gave him this journal." she said. "Read what I wrote inside it. I think you'll like it."

I took the journal from her and read the inscription:

If you are ever afraid, my love, of losing my love, and if not a prayer comes to you and God seems to have forsaken you, then say my name and recite a poem and I will be there. Every time. Always. With love, your Leyla

"That's beautiful," I said.

How he inspired those words within her I didn't know. But he did. And I was ashamed for the slight jealousy, the tinge of sadness that clouded my constricting heart.

"Read from it," I said as I saw that the journal made her happy.

She turned to the middle then to the last page where there was ink and then back to the middle. She looked up.

"The last time you were here, that night when he gave it to me, he had written this."

And she read, "*I have strange dreams. Dreams sometimes of being chased. Of falling. Of reaching up to the sky and not having anything to hold. These dreams are always there and with time there are other dreams of darkness or of too much light. And then there are dreams that I crave, the dreams where I dream of you. And of me. And we are happy somewhere although I don't ever see where we are. We are not at home or in any of the places we have shared. These are the dreams that I crave. But know that I have never craved, never wanted anyone but you.*"

She looked at me for approval. I nodded. She flipped some pages.

"*When you came home today, you smelled of the perfume you used to wear when I met you. I was not asleep but pretended to be because I didn't want you to see my eyes. You say my eyes change when I am not myself. And I wonder who I am sometimes, whether the eyes you love are those of a visiting angel and I am evil or if the eyes you dread are those of a visiting demon and I am good. I don't know. But you make me believe I am the eyes you love. You make me believe I*" *am better than the worst. And as you touched my head and I smelled your perfume, I remembered the small restaurant where we had our first date. How beautiful you looked. You wore red. A red dress that I adored. How you smelled when I hugged you. You smelled like that today. And it made me… it made me want to be better for you. I promise to take the meds every day no matter how much I hate it. I promise."*

She looked up at me.

"When he gets better," she began, "he sometimes skips his meds. It makes him go deeper into highs and lows when he does. And I hate it. I never understand why he stops. But he says when he feels better he feels he doesn't need them. It's so frustrating."

I listened. All I did was listen because I felt all I could do was listen. I had nothing to offer by way of words. This is not the life I had imagined for her. I had imagined Leyla as running through fields and having an easy love, an easy life. Part of me still wondered why she didn't. She could easily leave as she had done after Jay. But she chose to stay. And this baffled me.

"I love you," she read, *"I know our love has flaws. But just because we love imperfectly, it doesn't make that love less perfect. But still, I wish to be perfect for you."*

"He writes well," I said.

"He doesn't write to write. He talks to me. He pours himself into these pages. He never writes otherwise. And doesn't know how. He only knows how to talk to me through his journals. And it makes… and it makes everything better. Because otherwise, I don't know anything about what he thinks or feels."

I was, once again, at a loss for words. All I wondered was if this was really the way she wanted to live, through journals, through his ups and down, through his madness. Leyla had worlds awaiting her if she wished to pursue them.

"You're wondering why I stay with him?" she asked as if reading my mind.

"No. Well, yes. I mean you could have anyone."

"And what if I have someone who is also dealt a bad hand at life? Do I leave him too?"

I shifted on the couch.

"If the point is to have easy love then why," she asked softly, "then why do you still love me the way you do knowing it's impossible?"

I had no answer for Leyla.

Chapter Forty-Five

The next week brought with it snowstorms and sleet. Every time the door opened, it brought with it gusts of wind and chill. It was two days before Christmas and although we had been busier than usual the weeks prior and even the days prior, that day was slower and more languid, and Ed and Leyla and I enjoyed the calm.

A bit past noon an elderly man came in. His walker was jammed in the door and Ed helped him in. He presented Ed with a pair of glasses that must have been a decade old.

"These are my spares." he said. "Need a screw. But then don't we all?"

He laughed at his own joke and when Ed asked him to sit he said, "Nah. Couldn't get back up if I did."

Ed replaced the screw for him and handed him his glasses back.

"What do I owe ya, fella?"

"Nothing."

"Ah no, no charity here. Here, buy some coffee."

The man handed Ed a folded bill and by the looks of it, it would have seemed as if he slipped him a fortune. Ed placed it in his pocket and helped the man out.

"You rich now?" I joked as Ed closed the door.

"It's a dollar, kiddo. But I took it because I didn't

want him to feel bad. When I was your age, someone tried to hand me a dollar and I stepped back, and it fell. You know what she said? She said, 'I know it isn't anything and that's why you don't want to take it.' Hurt her feelings. Never refused a dollar since."

"Why is he out in this weather for a spare pair screw anyway?" I asked.

"Well, you heard him." Ed said as he gave me his lopsided smile. "Everyone needs a screw."

Leyla was standing against the wall eating a green apple and she laughed.

I saw Ed looking out of the window and knew he was debating going out for a snack despite the weather.

"Just order something," I suggested.

"When there's such good stuff right around the corner? Besides, they don't deliver frozen yogurt."

Leyla laughed again. She reminded me of the Leyla I had met by a pool table, full of life and possibilities.

"Guys, I wanted to ask you something," she said.

We both looked at her, waiting.

"How about you come over for Christmas? And Sam, of course. Raza feels bad about us cancelling on you guys on his account for dinner last week. He suggested we could all have a nice Christmas dinner. I'll even make biryani for Ed."

I thought of Raza as I had left him, on the couch watching reruns of old shows.

"I'll be there, Doc," Ed said.

"I'll be there as well," I said.

"As well." Leyla repeated and laughed slightly. "The way you speak sometimes. It's so… proper."

"And?" I retorted.

"And nothing. It's cute," she said as she walked to the front desk to place the apple core in the garbage.

"Your husband feeling better?" Ed asked.

"Much."

"We have to find you a husband, kiddo." Ed said. "What do you think, Doc? Your husband have any hot single friends?"

The room was drowned in silence and I waited. I wanted in some ways to swim to the surface, to tell Ed what I wanted. But there was a fear in me that kept me drowned. I wondered if I would ever swim, ever be free. Or perhaps I too would swing on a heavy rope someday unable to cope with the expectations and the life imposed upon me.

"Priya doesn't need me." Leyla said finally freeing me from all expectation. "She'll find someone to love."

Chapter Forty-Six

Ed and Sam and I left for Leyla's place together. She had left earlier and was expecting us. When we arrived, Ed was mesmerized by the building, the doorman and the gleaming floors of the lobby.

"Doc does well," he joked with Sam.

Sam grunted. He was dressed immaculately with a new charcoal suit and deep blue shirt and tie. Ed wore his sea foam green shirt again and I wondered why he ever chose not to have shirts and ties that fit as well when he could find them. When we arrived at the front, the doorman tipped his hat to me and let us pass.

"Seems like he knows you," Ed said.

I said nothing in response but led them to the elevator.

Once inside, the door shut, and I saw Ed fixing his tie in the mirrored door.

"Doc's got class, living here," he said.

Sam was smoothing back his hair with one hand. In the other he held a wine bottle in a golden wine bag.

Ed had brought a dozen red roses with baby's breath that I was holding. I tried to hand the bouquet back to him, but he ignored me as he kept fiddling with his tie.

"Take your flowers," I said as I felt strange about handing Leyla a dozen red roses.

"Give me a minute, kiddo."

As we ascended, Sam and Ed finally became satisfied or at least stopped fixing themselves. There was something about Leyla that made people want to be perfect for her. I knew this. I knew this because I usually felt inadequate in her presence no matter how well I tried to dress or which eyeliner I used. She was someone who elicited the desire to be perfect. I of all people knew she always had.

When we arrived at Leyla's door, Ed took his flowers and rang the bell. Almost instantly, Leyla answered, dressed in a striking red dress that ended just above her knees. She wore diamond earrings that dangled and caught the light, sparkling and glittering. Her pendant was also a single diamond, suspended from a thin silver chain.

"Hello, hello," she said.

We entered and stood in her foyer. She took the wine from Sam and the flowers from Ed.

"These are beautiful," she said.

Ed smiled feeling accomplished.

"Please, come in," Leyla said as she gestured towards the living room.

As we were entering the living room, I saw Raza standing by the couch, smiling. His beard was shaved clean and he looked almost boyish. He wore a perfectly crisp shirt with the top button open. He wore deep green khakis that were just as perfectly pressed, and his shoes were shiny brown wingtips that looked new. As I walked closer, I could smell his cologne, a delicious woodsy smell that I imagined Leyla must have loved. I glanced towards the couch hesitantly as if I would find Raza there as well, bearded and swaddled in a blanket.

But there was no Raza there. Raza was standing in front of me, vivacious and full of a life I hadn't seen him embrace in the past few times I had seen him.

"Welcome, friends," he said wholeheartedly.

We each took a seat, myself and Leyla on the couch, Sam and Ed on the twin armchairs across. Raza stood, looking at us, smiling.

"Thank you for joining me and my wife this evening," he said.

"*My wife.*" I repeated the words to myself, silently. I knew Leyla was his wife. But hearing him say it made it seem as if I had never known. I started wondering how it felt to claim someone. I had never had the luxury of doing so. I had, in the short-lived romance I had known, had her claim me as "her girlfriend" then "her fiancée" but I had always referred to her by name. I had never loved anyone enough to claim her and I never claimed Leyla as anything because saying "my best friend" seemed such a lie I couldn't bring myself to form the words.

I started to ache for someone I had never known. I started to ache to have someone open a door to me at the end of a day or to kiss my forehead to make any pain within my soul dissipate. I yearned for the whispers and dialogues and brief kisses and long lovemaking I had heard of and imagined Raza and Leyla to share. But I had never had it. Because more than any love I had had or known, I had known the phantom love of loving Leyla. As silly as it was, I began to resent her for it although it was I who stayed in love. It was bizarre really, this business of loving.

"What can I get you to drink?" Raza asked shattering my thoughts.

"I brought some wine," Sam said as he handed Raza the gold paper bag.

Raza took the bag and extracted the wine.

"This is a fine bottle," he said to Sam and Sam seemed pleased.

I watched him set the wine on the glass table. He left for a moment, came back with a fancy corkscrew and effortlessly opened the bottle. He went back again, and I saw he brought glasses, the stems neatly arranged between his fingertips.

"I used to bartend in college," he said.

"That's good money," Sam said.

"It was. It got me through a lot of rough patches."

As Raza poured wine, I felt Leyla tense next to me. I kept watching him pour and saw he had poured four even glasses and a fifth half glass.

"Merry Christmas," he said as he passed the glasses to us reserving the half glass for himself.

We drank in a comfortable silence. There was no haste that evening, there was no sadness or fear. Raza entertained us with story after story and I marveled at his ease, his charm. I looked to Leyla who winked at me with a smile and I believed that perhaps this was the way it would be from then on, that this is who Raza would be from then on. It was a naïve assumption, or one based in hope perhaps. But for Leyla's sake, I hoped that his eyes danced forever the way they did then in the light, perfectly full and balanced and happy.

Leyla had cooked an amazing dinner for us. When she laid the table, the fragrances of spices and meats was irresistible. Ed's eyes widened at the tray of chicken biryani before him and Sam eyed the goat curry with curiosity. There was plain rice pilaf and a vegetable medley as well as cucumber yogurt spiced with cumin.

"I hope you are hungry," Leyla said.

"I could eat everything on the table," Ed said.

"We know," Sam retorted.

"My wife is a great cook. The best," Raza said.

"Although Raza cooked the goat curry." Leyla replied. "He cooks the meats."

"Don't know what to do with a vegetable."

"My kind of guy," Sam said.

We sat at the table and began our meal.

"This is great." Ed said as he took a forkful of biryani to his mouth.

"It's nice to have a husband to help. Raza prepared the chicken for it."

"I was telling Priya." Ed said as he chewed. "We have to find her husband."

"Or a wife maybe," Leyla replied.

Ed stopped chewing for a moment.

Sam looked from Leyla to Ed to me.

I stared at Leyla and wondered how she had so nonchalantly laid my life on the table. If she had her secrets, her inadmissions, then I had mine too. The difference was, I kept my silences for her and I always had. It didn't matter why we kept parts of ourselves hidden, all that mattered was that we respected each other's decisions to do so. Her words were tinged with a betrayal I had never known nor anticipated. I had kept her life's secrets inside me while she had splayed mine out before me at a dinner table.

"The weather's gotten really cold," Raza offered by way of diffusing the conversation.

I played with a forkful of rice, unable to look

anywhere but my plate, unwilling to put the fork in my mouth.

"Excuse me," I said as I rose to go to the bathroom.

As I was turning the knob to the bathroom door, I heard footsteps on the hardwood.

"Priya," she said.

"What the fuck was that?"

I was facing her now, my eyes blazing as they looked into hers, her eyes reticent and hesitant in their gaze back.

"Priya I don't understand the big deal."

I was silent while I tried to snatch the correct words. Nothing came to me, so I stayed as I was, hand on the doorknob, my eyes locked with hers. The silence was taut and full and about to burst.

"This was not your story to tell," I finally said.

"Priya, I didn't mean to hurt you."

"You didn't hurt me. You betrayed me."

"How? I didn't lie."

If she had apologized then, asked for forgiveness, it would have been hers to take. But instead, she insisted, and I was losing my tolerance. To keep from screaming or worse crying, I entered the bathroom and shut the door.

I heard her footsteps shuffle outside for a long time.

Chapter Forty-Seven

Silence followed her betrayal. It wasn't as if we didn't talk when we were at 20/20 but when we did, it was optically related talk regarding a prescription when I couldn't decipher her handwriting or talk about a patient and what they might have bought. There was no tension between us and this bothered me because I felt there should be some repercussion, but none existed.

If Ed noticed that things were different between Leyla and me, he didn't say it nor show it. It was a languid winter day towards the end of January when I had just finished a sale and Ed was hovering behind me as he did when he was bored or, more often, hungry.

"Kiddo, I don't think you should be so hard on her," he finally said.

"Who?" I asked although my stomach somersaulted, and I knew who.

"The doc. I don't think she meant to hurt you."

"She betrayed me."

"We're family, kiddo."

I turned and looked up at his tall, looming frame.

"It wasn't her story to tell."

"It's not a story. It's part of who you are. And the last thing the doc would do is hurt anyone."

"How do you know that?"

"She's good people, kiddo."

I felt my face flush and it was as if Ed were taking her side. I didn't know how to defend myself anymore, so I stayed quiet, shuffling trays and pretending to concentrate. He cleared his throat.

"I'm going out for a snack," he announced.

As Ed left and the bells jangled, I wondered if Ed was right or if I was. I still didn't think she should have said what she said but what really kept me angry was her nonchalance, her refusal to even entertain the possibility that she had done something wrong.

I was about to rise from my chair when she walked onto the sales floor.

"Hey, Priya. You alone out here?"

"Ed went for a snack."

She sauntered to the dispensing counter and stood crossing her arms.

"How are you?"

"You see me every day. I'm fine."

"Priya, you can't still be angry."

"Why not?"

"Because it wasn't that big of a deal. And—"

"Not that big of a deal? You still don't see it, do you? You just don't see it. Why—"

"And because I'm sorry."

My eyes met hers and for some reason I didn't know it was as if I were back in college and my stomach fluttered and turned and I felt again, as if I so often had, regardless of her words or actions, that my own resolve melted, and everything was okay because it was her and she could never do wrong. The hold she had on me hadn't lifted after all this time and I wondered if she would and could always make me feel as if everything was okay with just a wayward glance or a meeting of the eyes.

She had this magic that I knew I would never be able to pull apart and understand. If it was a slight of hand then I tried so hard to follow the motions, to unravel her, to finally have a moment where I could say, "Aha! That's how you do it." But such a moment had never been because as I looked into her eyes I stopped wondering about the magic and became entirely consumed by it.

She blinked now and then but did not take her gaze away from mine. I shamelessly drank from her eyes, tried to enter her through her gaze and wondered for the first time what it would be like if she could look at me always. I wondered what it would be like to be Raza, to be enveloped by that gaze and to hold it again and again. Finally, she smiled, and she looked perfect and I felt a jealousy towards him that I couldn't fathom I had. I had snatches of that smile back then and sometimes now, but I could imagine that he saw that smile often, in moments of intimacy when they shared whispers or wine.

I had never known jealousy to be such a fierce animal. Inside my chest, there was a dull pain when I thought of Raza and her together. I knew it was wrong to think so but I felt it from my clenching fists to my shallow breath to my curling toes. I had never known anything so overwhelming and it frightened me as it gripped me hard and would not let go.

"Are you okay?" she asked.

Before I could answer, Ed burst in with frozen yogurt. The jangle of bells broke whatever spell was cast and jealousy retreated like a wounded fox into the cavern of my soul. I knew it would return and it scared me, the power of it, the sheer ugliness of it. I looked down at the floor and tried to pretend that for the moment just before, I hadn't become a beast in the ways that I wanted her.

Chapter Forty-Eight

It was a dreary Tuesday when I walked into 20/20 soaked, my umbrella limp and broken in my hand as I pushed the door open. Ed turned from the counter where he was checking jobs and whistled.

"You look like you've been through a war," he said.

"This damn weather," I said as I threw the umbrella to the floor.

"Well come in and dry up. And oh, no doctor today."

"Why?" I asked.

"She said she isn't feeling too well. Settle in and then reschedule the appointments for today I guess."

He turned back to the lensometer and continued checking jobs. I watched him for a moment as he hunched over with an eye to the eyepiece, the other eye squinting. His massive hands turned the power drum with ease and he breathed audibly as he worked. I wondered what thoughts were within him and then accepted that he probably thought only of the work before him, diopters and pupillary distances and segment heights. Whereas my head constantly veered towards randomness, feelings and ideas that ricocheted off the walls of my mind, I was somehow sure Ed's mind didn't work like that. I started to wonder if anyone's mind worked like that.

I went into the office and flicked on the light. The room was stale, and I focused on the coffee rings on the desk. I was trying, I knew, to focus on anything and everything except Leyla.

I had had a dream the night before. We were here, at 20/20, in her office. She had just finished an exam and she was writing notes at her desk. The lights were still off, EVOT shining boldly on the bright screen on the wall. I walked in and cleared my throat. She looked up.

"Your next appointment is here."

She rose from her chair, her skirt billowing around her shins. She walked past me and closed the door, without a word, soundlessly.

"Priya," she said.

And then she leaned and brushed my lips with the back of her hand. And then she kissed me.

That was the dream, the whole dream. It wasn't that I woke up and there was more. That was the entire dream and then there was no dream, no image, just sleep.

"What do you think is wrong with her?"

I jumped at Sam's voice behind me.

"I don't know," I said honestly. "Bad Chinese food?"

He let out a gruff "whatever" and walked around me to the desk.

"She's killing my bottom line, my margin."

"Sam, I'm sure she'll be back tomorrow."

"You didn't hear?"

"What?"

He squinted, and the corners of his eyes creased.

He leaned back in his chair and put his hands behind his head.

"She called. She won't be in for the week. The week, Priya. What kind of joke is this? There isn't Chinese food bad enough for that."

"I'll go see what's up if you want."

I don't know why I said it all in a rush like that but the thought of no Leyla for a week made me want to see her despite the dream. Or maybe because of it.

"Would you? I mean it's not protocol but if you could find out what's going on... ."

"I'll go after work."

"Go now. Hell, there's no one in here. And Ed and I can handle it."

"Now?"

"Why not?"

I looked at the walls, an old calendar hung above Sam's head, the dates all wrong and the edges of the pages curled loosely.

"Will you go, Priya?"

He was pleading more than asking. I looked at him and wondered if he dreamt of 20/20 in ways that I dreamt of Leyla. If the only lover he knew or cared for was brick and mortar, if he had given up on skin and breath and preferred this obsessive love affair with a thing, with a business, with his own bottom line and profit and loss analysis.

I waved to him and walked out of the room. I retrieved my umbrella although, upon looking outside, I realized it was cloudy, but the rain had stopped.

"Where you off to, kiddo?"

He had his eye to the eyepiece and didn't even turn around.

"To see Leyla."

He didn't answer me but I saw his head move slightly as if in a nod, still hunched over the lensometer.

The air smelled wilted, as if the rain had made everything stale. I walked to the subway and while I should have been wondering what I would say when I saw her or how I would explain myself, I could think only of the feel of her mouth and the darkness behind my eyes as she kissed me.

Chapter Forty-Nine

"And who are you?"

The doorman peered at me over the glasses perched mid nose on his face. I hadn't seen this doorman before. For a foolish instant, I missed the doorman I knew, the one who recognized me. It was a moment of wanting to feel I belonged in her building, in her apartment, in her life and most intimate of moments. I felt out of place and was restless.

"Priya," I managed to say.

"Is Dr. Ibrahim expecting you?"

"Yes," I lied.

He coughed slightly as he held a phone to his ear. I heard it ring three times. And then her voice.

"Hello?"

"Yes, a Priya is here to see you. Shall I send her up?"

Silence.

He held the phone away and coughed again.

"Yes, send her up please."

"All right then. Very well."

He nodded, and I walked towards the elevators, my reflection seeming heavy upon the closed doors. Now I wondered what I would say, how I would explain myself, what I would ask.

The doors opened, and I entered. As they shut, I was confronted with my reflection again.

When I reached her apartment, she was in the doorway, half leaning out, her feet still firm in her own space.

"Priya, are you okay?"

"Am *I* okay? I came to see if you were okay."

She moved to let me in. As I passed her in the doorway, I caught a slight hint of jasmine. When I entered, I was enveloped in jasmine, the incense burning deep and strong at an unseen altar.

"Priya, have a seat."

We walked to the couch and sat as if this visit was nothing out of the ordinary. Although it was mid-afternoon and neither of us should have been there. But we were.

"Why aren't you at work?" she asked.

"I could ask the same of you."

She let out a deep breath that I didn't even realize she was holding.

"Raza is not too well. He had anxiety attacks all night and I can't leave him by himself. It happens. I have a doctor's appointment for him tomorrow. We have to see about changing medication, adding medication, I don't know."

Her gaze was resigned although she looked at me, her eyes meeting mine but focused on some other thought or place. I tried not to look at her mouth. Not because it was slightly quivering, waiting for her to let tears fall but because I could swear I remembered the sensation of it although it was only a dream. I was slightly ashamed for my thoughts and yet they wouldn't subside.

"Leyla, if there is anything I can do, tell me."

Here she let a tear slip from the corner of her right eye as she looked up at the ceiling. Here, she opened her mouth slightly and said, "Sometimes, I just can't anymore." And I wished she didn't love him as she did. But she did. And I knew that she did. And that made the ache of wishing for her that much more.

"What can I do?" I asked as I wiped the tear from her eye and let me hand rest softly at her jaw.

"Nothing. No one can do anything."

I stared at the crimson painting on the wall and tried to read the Rumi inscribed in the square.

"He's sleeping," she said.

I nodded. I took my hand from her face and she grabbed my hand, held it and wouldn't let it go. Her skin felt soft and her fingers felt beautiful against my palm. Her tattoo glowed a soft black and orange and I caught myself reciting "OM."

She leaned her head against my shoulder and we sat there wordless. Her energy was as spent, as defeated as when we lay in a bed once, my hand across her empty abdomen, speaking of anything but what we knew to be the reason for her grief. On her couch, I moved slightly, and she looked up at me. I don't know what moved inside me, I don't know if it was courage or lust or confusion, but I leaned over and my lips softly brushed hers.

She jumped, and I fell back onto the couch. She was standing over me, her eyes ablaze but I don't know with which emotion exactly.

"Priya!"

I could almost feel her heartbeat across the space that was between us, her leaning over me and me thrown back onto the couch cushions.

"I—I-"

I myself didn't know what that was. I didn't know from whence it came or what I was trying to do. Years of knowing her and never having betrayed her. Except now. But was it a betrayal really? Was it so bad to have kissed someone or to have tried to or to have—

"Baby."

Raza's gruff voice entered the room before he did. He was all stubble and tossed hair and the sight of him made me burn with envy.

She walked to him effortlessly, smiled and then. And then she kissed him fully, the arch of her lips fitting upon his perfectly. I watched their kiss and burned like fire. Why did he deserve her when I had loved her much before, had been there in times he didn't even know? Why did she love him despite his madness, despite the trouble of it all?

I watched her take his hand, lead him to the couch. He sat, and I could tell he was disoriented. I could tell he was kind of a shell and whatever was inside him had become lost.

She leaned down and met his eyes with hers. Then, when she looked into him, his shell became filled with being, with a person, and the hint of charming Raza surfaced again. I didn't marvel at the power of her gaze. I had known it many times, that look in her eyes that could make the heart beat faster, make the soul want to be alive and feel and tumble and love all over again.

"Priya?"

She said my name as if nothing had changed except I knew it had.

"Priya, I'm going to go get us all some lunch. The place Raza likes doesn't deliver. Will you stay with him please?"

"Sure."

Without even a question or glance to acknowledge my curt response, she went to the bedroom, came back with a purse, her phone in her hand, and left.

I sat next to the love of her life imagining again and again the ease with which her mouth kissed his. And then my mind traveled, quite unwillingly, to the feel of her lips against mine. I looked at the mess that he was and wondered why and how I wasn't good enough to be loved.

Chapter Fifty

We must have not spoken or spoken while she was away but the only dialogue that comes to mind is this:

"How are you, Priya?" he said slowly, stressing every syllable.

"I am great. How are you?"

"I have been better."

"I see that."

I didn't see the point in politeness.

"Priya, you know Leyla. You know her well."

I looked at him and he looked tired, haggard almost. But when he spoke of Leyla, his eyes ignited with grace.

"Yes, I know her."

"Does she love me, Priya?"

He looked at me with eyes that were pleading for some affirmation. Even he knew then that he wasn't deserving of her love, that she deserved someone who could love her wholly without madness or grief or the stupidity of having to ask a virtual stranger to affirm her affection.

One word can change destiny.

And so, it was fated perhaps.

"No," I said.

I saw a man crumble to nothingness as he trembled and wept.

I did not stop him as he went to the door and turned the knob and exited.

Chapter Fifty-One

I returned to 20/20 as if I hadn't just left chaos in my wake. I should have followed Raza, brought him back to the apartment. Or at the very least I should have waited until Leyla returned. But I did neither. I instead left quietly, shutting the door behind me and took the train back.

Chapter Fifty-Two

The skies tore apart and rained heavy, hefty drops onto the pavement. I refused to open my umbrella although it was slack in my hand. I thought only of Raza's face, his limp walk, his exit. I thought then of her mouth on his, how perfectly it fit, then the feel of her lips as they brushed mine. Fragments of thoughts collided and slid in my mind until I stopped walking, threw my slack umbrella to the ground and closed my eyes.

Had I really done anything? He would probably sulk and walk until he turned and returned back home. Home. His home. Her home. Their home. When the only home I knew was her. When the only home I wanted her to know was me. But she had taken him whole. His art, his being, his name. *Ibrahim.* The consonants sounded jagged and harsh on my tongue.

When I opened my eyes, the rain caused the world to blur. It beat hard with a rhythm all its own. A shard of lightening cracked the sky in two and I felt, right there, that something was very wrong.

Chapter Fifty-Three

When I walked into 20/20 an hour later, Sam was sitting across from a young couple and was urging them to try high definition lenses. Ed was on the phone ordering lenses, a stack of trays beside him. I walked quietly to the office. I set my phone on the desk. Then I sat on Sam's chair and felt the world spin. I was soaked and shivered with cold. My phone started to vibrate moving slightly on the desk. I knew before I looked down that it would be her calling. I let it vibrate helplessly and didn't pick up. It stopped. Again, it vibrated and moved in a buzz on the desk. Again, I did not pick up.

I heard Sam's heavy footsteps before he entered the office.

"So?" he asked.

"So?"

"Well you were gone a while. And why are you soaked? Umbrella break?"

"Something like that. But I did talk to her. She won't be back for the week."

"What's wrong with her?"

I shrugged. I didn't know how to answer him.

"That's what you went over there to find out? That's what you found out?"

Divya Sood

"Sam, I am not her keeper. I don't know. All she said was she wouldn't be back. I didn't even go in. We spoke at the door."

I swallowed after the lie.

"And that took you all this time?"

"What do you want me to say, Sam? The weather is terrible and I got stuck in the rain. If you want answers from her, ask her."

He sighed deeply with disappointment.

"Why don't you go home?" he finally said.

"What?"

"You're soaked. You can't work like that. Ed and I will take care of it today."

"Fine."

"And Priya?"

"Yes?"

My gaze met his.

"If you're going to lie to me, it'd be better to just tell me to mind my fucking business."

He turned and slammed the door before I could offer a response.

Chapter Fifty-Four

After I got home and changed into a dry T-shirt and jeans, I called her. I didn't call her because I had to. I called her because I wanted to hear her voice.

"Priya?" she almost jumped at me.

"Hey Leyla."

"Priya, is Raza with you?"

"No."

"Then?"

Her voice was stuck there at "then," an infinite question hanging and looming in the air. I didn't answer because there is no answer to the word "then."

"Priya, where is Raza?"

Her concern infuriated me.

"How the hell should I know where your husband is?"

I said husband as if it were a dirty word, one that was foul and base and not to be used.

"Priya, what happened? Did you leave him alone?"

"I got a call from Sam, so I had to leave."

"You could have waited until I got home. I asked you to stay with him because he is not well. Where will I look for him?"

"How the hell should I know?"

"What is the matter with you?"

233

I could imagine the fury in her eyes.

"Priya?"

"I have to get back to work."

"You're not at work. I called Sam."

"Then I have to get back to something else. Raza is not my concern, Leyla."

"But he is mine," she said softly, and I realized before I knew it that she had hung up the phone.

Chapter Fifty-Five

I picked up the phone and dialed his number. I don't know what made me do it. But it was after 2:00 in the morning and I had had a dream where he asked, "When are you coming to Calcutta?" I dreamt just once sentence in a snippet of a dream and I awoke in a panic, upright and barely breathing. I picked up the phone and dialed his number not realizing for that flash of an instant that he wouldn't pick up.

"Hello?"

Aasthika.

"Hello?"

"Priya?"

"Yes. Yes. I—"

"Why didn't you come for the cremation?"

This was the most I had ever heard from her, these seven words, and I had no answer to her question.

"I—" I started and then swallowed. The air was thin, and my head was swimming with thoughts of him and somewhere in her sphere a baby started to cry and somewhere in her world someone was comforting the baby and she was still waiting for me to answer.

"He would have wanted you there," she said.

"You don't know what he wanted," I said without

realizing the sound of it. Without awareness that I was speaking to Prem's wife. I had never thought of her as part of him and yet they had created life. They had shared time and space and moments that were theirs alone. And yet I had never accepted her as part of him.

There was silence and I waited. I wanted her to offer me something that told me she loved him. I wanted to know that he was loved although I could never be sure whether he loved back.

"Raj," she said.

"I'm sorry?"

"His name is Raj."

"Whose name?" I asked impatiently.

She was silent.

"What are you talking about?" I asked.

"The one he loved. His name is Raj."

It was my turn to contemplate in silence, to weigh each of the eight words she said. And then, in turn, I had questions, more questions than there could be answers for. I wished I hadn't called. I wished he hadn't called out in a dream that compelled me to want to speak to him, to hear, just once, his voice asking when I would come to Calcutta with the subtle subtext of why I had forsaken him after his wedding, a wedding he had tolerated and endured but had no desire for. I swallowed.

"Aasthika—" It was the first time I had addressed her. It was the first time I said her name. And it felt foreign.

There was a long silence to follow.

Silence followed silence.

When she hung up, I clung to the phone, listening to nothingness.

Chapter Fifty-Six

I wasn't sleeping when I heard the buzzer. I lazily walked to the door and opened it.

Leyla.

Leyla shining with rain, her lips pink and quivering as if she were trying to form words. Leyla as beautiful as she was in person, in my thoughts, in all the dreams I ever had.

Here she was at my threshold once again coming to me and yet never mine.

"Priya, I don't know what to do. Where to go."

I didn't move or talk. Didn't invite her in with actions or words. But she took a step forward, pushed me gently to the side and walked, once again, into my life.

"Priya, what do I do? He's not home."

I wanted to tell her I really didn't care for this but then I looked at her and although it could have just been rainwater, I knew she was crying because of the unevenness of her breath, the redness of her eyes.

She moved to me, held me and I felt the water seep into my shirt, cool my skin. I thought back to how many times she had held me through her pain and yet never once held me through mine. The pain of knowing her, of wanting her, of betraying her was never shared, never explored, never exploded into our lives. And yet she was Leyla. And I was Priya. And once again, I couldn't turn her away but only offer her solace, my soul, my love.

"Leyla, we will get through this. We will find him."

"What if something happens to him?"

Here she pulled away, looked deep and penetratingly into my eyes so much so that I had to look away lest she see that I had caused her this pain. That for once, I wasn't just her comfort, I was the cause of her distress.

"We'll find him." I said.

I didn't know how or where or when we would find him. But I knew she wanted to hear that we would. So, I said it. Words sometimes are not truthful but a balm to heal fear and worry.

"Where will I even go?"

"Police?" I offered.

"No!"

Her emphatic answer made me step back.

"Just that they might hurt him."

"Why would they hurt him?"

"Priya he's not well. He will act crazy. They don't have tolerance for crazy."

"I think you're overreacting."

"Priya," she whispered, and I imagined her whisper as one of want of me instead of despair over the one she truly loved.

"Priya," she said again and this time I shook my head clear and waited for what she was about to say.

"Did you see him? He's a mess. And he is unwell. The last thing I want is for the police to seek out my husband, my unwell Muslim husband, and hurt him because they can and no one will question it. Do you understand how scared I am? Do you understand that I don't even know what to do?"

She collapsed into me, her head on my shoulder, the scent of her shampoo lingering and her sobs loud and desperate. I felt my stomach churn because it was the first time I realized not only how scared she was but also how right she was about the futility of the situation I had created. I wished Raza would just return partly because of worry but mostly because of guilt.

Chapter Fifty-Seven

We slept the night next to each other. We didn't sleep but lay, her head on my shoulder, her arm across my torso, my attempted kiss untalked of and flung into oblivion. How many times we had been like this, her in despair, me her solace? Yet this time instead of drinking in her presence and desiring her, I was filled with a confusion I had never known. Was I not the reason we were here? If something were to happen to Raza, would I, could I forgive myself? Fear draped a sorry arm over me and I moved, twitched almost.

"Are you, all right?"

"Yes," I lied.

"Do you remember back then, when I was afraid, you would recite verses of the *Chalisa* for me?"

"I remember."

"Can you do it again? Because I am terrified."

She nuzzled into me and her arm became tighter around me. I started the *Chalisa* from the beginning, searching in the rhythm of the couplets for some courage, some indication that everything would turn out just fine.

Her phone rang long and deep into the night.

She jumped out of the bed. She retrieved her phone. She picked up.

"Hello?" she said.

Tum rakshak kahoo ko darna?

If you are my keeper, then why be afraid?

"This is Leyla, yes. Dr. Ibrahim."

Bhoot pisach nikat nahin avai

Mahabir jab naam sunavai

No ghosts or demons ever come

When Hanuman announces his name

"I… I will be there soon. Yes. Yes… yes."

She hung up.

"Raza," she said more to him than to me as if he could hear her across this expanse of time and space. As if he were tied to her.

"Raza?" I asked.

"They found him."

"Who found him? Where?"

"The police found him unconscious. Beaten. They found my number as the last he had dialed on his phone. He's in the hospital. He is still unconscious. That is all I know."

She slumped onto the couch and I saw her crying in waves, in trembles, in fear. I took her hand.

Chapter Fifty-Eight

When we arrived at the hospital, I was not allowed to
see Raza as he was in the ICU and only family was
allowed in. There were officers there in their crisp blue
assaulting Leyla with questions. She seemed frail, yet
she held her strength. Now that I think back, I realize
she could have told them that I was the last to see him
before he left the apartment. Yet she never did. The
only thing she mentioned was going out to get food,
leaving him in the apartment, coming home to the
place empty.

I waited outside, pacing as she went and saw him,
talked to him I assumed although I knew he was
unconscious, sat with him, spoke to his doctors. The
story followed that someone walking by stopped to call
the police when they found Raza unconscious near a
garbage bin somewhere in Soho. Most walked by him
but some guy who noticed blood called the police. The
police did not find anyone nearby who saw what
happened nor could they say what might have happened.
It seemed as though he were attacked for reasons other
than money as his phone was not touched. He had not
had his wallet with him.

Although this was enough for me, it definitely was
not for Leyla. She asked question after question, first of

the doctors who had no answers to her satisfaction and then of the police who had no answers either. It seemed that loss of blood was a concern and so was a massive concussion. What concerned Leyla most was that whoever attacked him had broken his hand.

"You're worried about his hand?" I asked.

"He's an artist, Priya."

I thought back to the paintings adorning their walls, to scribbles of Rumi and Hafiz. I looked at her and wanted to tell her somehow what I had done, why we were all here, how I had failed us. But I never did. Instead, I allowed her to lean on me as her eyes closed and she slipped into a soft sleep.

Chapter Fifty-Nine

When Raza gained consciousness, Leyla was still sleeping on my shoulder. I gently awakened her.

"Raza is awake," I said.

His name felt so wrong in my mouth.

She rose quickly and went to him.

I sat and recited the Chalisa again from memory. Again. And again.

When Leyla finally came back to me, I got up from my chair.

"He's hurt," she said as if she hadn't realized this the night before.

"I know."

"I don't mean that, Priya. The first thing he asked me was 'Do you love me?' Why would he ask me that? Did I not love him well enough? Does he not know? How could he ask me that? Is that why he wandered off? Is that why this happened?"

How could I tell her that this happened not because she didn't love him but because I loved her? And love, as beautiful as we believe it is, has a twisted, baser side, a side that invokes not art and poems but jealous demons and rage? How could I ever explain to her that this all happened in spite of her love and because of mine? And if I did, what would come of it?

I let her grief fall into me, folded it into a perfect square and tucked it within me like a handkerchief meant for tears.

"Priya, I love him."

Four words that burned within my heart. As true as they were. As untrue as I wanted them to be. The perfect words, I knew, never to be uttered by her were, "Priya, I love you."

Chapter Sixty

Raza returned home eight days after the morning in the hospital when Leyla said, "Priya, I love him."

I was at work, adjusting a stubborn zyl frame when Ed told me the phone was for me. I glared at him wondering why he would interrupt me with a patient problem when I was already dealing with one.

"It's Leyla," he said as if he had read my thoughts.

My thoughts sank into my stomach and the somersaults that resulted made my hands shake. I put the frame down and took the phone.

"Hello?"

"Priya, he's home."

Her voice surged with a current of relief. My body felt jealousy that rose and fell like electricity. And then I was washed in shame.

"I'm glad," I said.

I wondered on a whim if he had told her the truth of that day, my words, his silent submission to what he believed to be truth.

"How is he?"

"He's okay. He's not okay but he's recovering. His hand… "

"His hand?"

"I hope he can paint. That's what he keeps asking. That's what concerns him."

"Did they find who assaulted him?"

"No. And I don't really think they care. And I don't. I just need his hand to be okay. So, he can paint for me again."

"Paint for me."

The words stuck in my ears, struck some chord. Paint for her. Use his hands upon her. With her, to hold her, to hold her hand, to create art not for the sake of art but for her. How she loved him. And how I loved her.

"Priya?"

"I have a patient. I have to go."

I hung up and gave Ed the phone. My hands still shook as I adjusted the frame, the woman in front of me breathing perilously through thin nostrils, wondering if I was going to break her precious Celine.

"All done," I said as I cleaned the lenses and handed the frames back to her.

She set them on her fragile nose and peered at me through the magnified lenses.

"They fit the same as when I gave them to you," she said as she rose, and, in a single motion, stormed to the door and burst out, the bells wild in their jangling.

I might have been upset except that I knew, given the circumstances, that she was 100 percent correct.

Chapter Sixty-One

"It's a shame what happened to her husband," Sam was saying. "But I don't understand why she wants to quit. I man the guy's okay now, isn't he?"

"Quit?"

"She called me and said she is not going to be working here anymore. I tried to talk to her, but she wouldn't give me the chance. These doctors. They're all loony."

Here, he leaned back in his chair and placed his hands behind his head. I knew what was to come from him next.

"Priya, if you could maybe talk to her?"

"What would I say, Sam?"

He shrugged as he lurched forward and sat up.

"I don't know. But you know her. And she listens to you."

"You want me to beg her to stay?"

"Not beg. Just suggest maybe? Please? For me?"

"What don't I do for you, Sam?" I asked, and I knew that he knew I would talk to Leyla.

"I'll call her."

"No, don't call her, see her. This has to be a face to face."

"I'll try."

Sam joined his hands as if in prayer.

"Thank you, Priya. You save me again."

"I haven't done anything yet. And we don't know if she'll stay anyway."

"I believe in you. And I believe that if you talk to her, she'll stay."

Chapter Sixty-Two

We meet at a Starbuck's café. We sit by the window, sunlight streaming onto our table. She sips her coffee, contemplating, and smiles warmly, her hands encircling her paper cup, the green Starbuck logo glowing under her intertwined fingers.

"How are you?" I ask.

She nods in response.

Silence as we looked at each other.

"Thank you for being there with me, for me, through everything," she finally offers.

I swallow a lump of guilt and it becomes lodged in my throat.

"Sam tells me you won't be coming back to work."

"I won't."

"Why?"

She sighs and looks at me as if she is noticing me.

I swallow some coffee too fast and although it sears my throat as it goes down, it takes with it the lump of guilt.

"Priya, Raza and I are leaving New York."

"But why?"

"Because."

"That's not an answer."

I look away and then back at her.

"It was my fault," I finally say.

She doesn't seem surprised and offers no reaction except to take a sip of her coffee.

"It was no one's fault."

"But I -"

"It was no one's fault. Or if it was, it was mine."

I look at her now and she places her hand on mine.

"Yours?"

She opens her mouth to speak, closes it again, her pink lips pressed together as if she is holding the words back.

"What is it?" I ask.

"For I love and this love was your gift."

"St. Augustine?"

"Yes. From Confessions."

"I don't understand."

Her hand presses against my skin.

"It was my fault that I asked so much of you back then, now, knowing you would give, knowing how much you love me. Knowing also I would never give back. That was, is my fault."

I blurt the sentence all at once: "I told Raza you didn't love him. I did that. That's why he left. And I didn't stop him."

She doesn't look away.

"And you did that because you hurt. Because whenever I enter your life, I bring pain to you. The pain of love, not the fulfillment of it."

"You knew?"

She takes her hand from mine and places it back on the coffee cup.

"I didn't know exactly. Raza never said anything."

"Then?"

"Then... then what? Then I need to leave you. I need you to live a life where you can find someone to love who loves you. Who doesn't make a dirty word of it by drawing you close and then nothing."

"It's not like that."

"It's exactly like that."

"So, you're not leaving 20/20. You're leaving me?"

"Yes."

I sit back and for no reason tears sting my eyes. It is as if we are going through a breakup although no relationship exists. Except that I love her. And she finally tells me that she will never love me. Not that I didn't know. But to hear it so solidly breaks my broken heart.

She rises to leave.

I stay seated.

She comes to my side of the table. I look up at her and she grazes my cheek with the back of her hand. Her hand remains on my face and I relish the softness of it, the warmth of her.

"Priya, you were my best friend. For what it's worth to you, I do love you for all we have endured."

I close my eyes so I do not have to watch her walk away. She removes her hand and I want to say, "Don't. Just wait like this, touch me again. Don't leave."

I say nothing.

When I open my eyes, she is not in the café.

"Leyla." I say aloud.

There is no answer, no solace.

Leyla. She is a fusion of all she knows, those she has seen and touched and tasted. I know now that I am a part of her experience on this earth, that she cannot extricate me from her being.

"*I do matter,*" *I say.*

I cannot simply be unraveled and thrown in a dustbin. If I carry the weight of her name within me etched in desire onto the parchment of my soul, then she also carries me within her perhaps not in the same way but in some way. Desire, unlike intimacy, does not need a partner and can be an eternal one-sided dance. I danced for her then and a part of me will always dance for her, regardless of the loves to come. Leyla.

About the Author

Divya Sood is the author of two novels: *Nights Like This* and *Maya*. *Find Someone to Love* is her third novel.

Divya studied Creative Writing and English at Rutgers University. While at Rutgers, she was awarded the NJ Chapter of Arts and Letters First Prize for Fiction, the Edna N. Herzberg First Prize for Fiction, and the Edith Hamilton First Prize for Fiction.

Divya pursued graduate work and earned a Master of Arts in English from New York University (NYU).

Divya has attended the Breadloaf Writers Conference.

Divya currently teaches at Gotham Writers Workshop in New York City, and is an adjunct professor of Creative Writing at Southern New Hampshire University (SNHU).

Website:www.div.nyc

Other Riverdale Avenue Books/Magnus Titles You Might Enjoy

Nights Like This
By Divya Sood

Blue Talk and Love
By Mecca Jamilah Sullivan

The Story of L
By Debra Hyde

Growing Up Golem:
How I Survived My Mother, Brooklyn ands Some
Really Bad Dates
By Donna Minkowitz